Betrayed:

She Was My Best Friend

By Dani K

This is a work of fiction. All characters, organizations, and events portrayed in this novel are either a product of the author's imagination or are used fictitiously. Any resemblance to actual persons, living or dead, is purely coincidental.

©2020 Brand Bullies INC/ Brand Bullies Publishing

All rights reserved. No part of this book may be reproduced or transmitted in any form without written permission from the author. With the exception to reviewers, magazine articles, newspapers, and radio hosts who have permission, which may quote brief passages for public display.

Sale of this book without a front cover may be unauthorized. If this book is coverless, it may have been reported to the publisher as "unsold or destroyed" and neither the author nor the publisher may have received payment for it.

Chapter 1

"I'm pregnant," Jewel said. Carefully studying Bankroll's facial expression and body language. He barely moved a muscle and didn't even blink. It was like his mind was gone and he was in daze.

"Nigga did you hear me? I'm pregnant!" Jewel shouted, this time with a more of an attitude than before.

Then diner grew extremely quiet and everyone around them had their eyes on Jewel. Bankroll gazed at Jew as she sat with her arms folded. Snapping out of his daze, Bankroll slammed his fist on the table just as he stood up.

"Bitch what?!" he screamed. "Ain't no way your triflin ass is pregnant by me!"

Jewel rolled her eyes. No matter how loud this nigga got it didn't faze her. Deep down inside

Jewel knew the love that Bankroll had for her. The roughness he displayed was to protect his tough boy image.

"What you mean *ain't no way I'm pregnant by you?"* Jewel held her composure as she looked straight into Bank's eyes. "You heard what I said. Nobody has time for these little games."

Jewel folded her arms as she leaned back in the booth they shared. Her pretty brown skin glowing from the sun beaming through the window. Her beautiful blue eyes could memorize you at any given moment to be not. Jewel was one of the most beautiful girls of her time, and Bankroll knew it.

Never having met anyone with her beauty, Bankroll was in love. Her body was golden. Jewel's slim-thick frame allowed her ass and titties to go perfect with her frame. Her skin smooth as silk and Melanin pop. Jewel was made perfect.

Bankroll just couldn't fight the urge to stay away from Jewel despite the rumors. Notorious for breaking men's hearts, Jewel prided herself on never giving her heart to anyone. Bank knew this.

His manhood would rise just at the sound of her voice. Wrapped around her pretty little finger, Bankroll took good care of Jewel. Never wanting for anything.

Jewel's beauty would often cloud his judgement. Spending endless money on her, giving her way too much access to things he shouldn't have. Jewel knew his game inside out. There have been times when Bankroll would grow suspicious, but never had any proof that he knew her ways we're scandalous, but he loved her.

Being pregnant by a dope boy was the "on the come up" scheme and it seemed like every bitch wanted a piece. Bankroll's lifestyle did allow him to have all types of women come and go. It seemed like anytime him and Jewel would be on the outs there was always a new one on his arm.

For years he avoided the baby mama hype. He was a true bachelor living his beat life with no responsibilities.

"Look, Jewel, I hear you all, but I'm not about to jump up and down in this motherfucking just because you say you knock up," Bankroll said as he sat back down. "You got to come better than that."

Jewel sat there as she stared at him, thinking of her next words carefully. Feeling enraged just at the thought of him really trying to play her like she had time to waste.

Jewel was a born hustler just like Bank. She knew the fame and knew there was no time to be wasted. Time was money, his money at that.

"Nigga you think I got time to be sitting up telling you I missed my period. I got better shit I could be doing," Jewel slid her shades on as she pulled out her iPhone.

Notifications booming left and right with Licks she needed to catch. Her best friend Lena was waiting for her call. Force to fend for herself, Jewel knew how to survive. Her Mimi taught how to be her own boss. Using her own goods.

"Baby girl I'm keeping it real with you." Her *Mimi would say. "You got to use what you got to her what you want! And never let a man make you fall in love."*

With those words instilled in her, Jewel lived by them daily. She eventually recruited her two best friends, Lena and Audra. Together they took the city of Columbia by storm ruining one of the biggest whore houses the south has ever seen.

No one knew Jewel was the boss but her two main bitches. She used the two to do her dirty work as she sat back and capitalized off it all. Lena and Audra never seem to complain. They knew wherever Jewel made it in life they would be right by her side making bank.

When Jewel first met Bankroll, she often confided in him how she one day wanted her own hair line and salon business. On their fourth date,

Bankroll blessed her with the money to do so. He invested in her dream as well as the girls.

Just like any other bitch. Jewel took the money and legalized her business without Bankroll knowing a thing.

Money was calling and being hustler just like him, Jewel had real moves to make. There was no time to be sitting up in Jackson's all you can eat buffet trying to prove to this nigga she was carrying a baby. His baby at that.

Letting out a deep breath, Jewel reached for her Louis Vuitton bag and pulled out paper towels and unwrapped the positive pregnancy test. Bankroll's face filled with disgust once he noticed the plastic stick.

"Man, I know you are not out here carrying around a pregnancy test in that eight hundred dollar bag I just bought yo ass," Bank was annoyed.

"Just look at it" Jewel shoved it toward him.

Silence grew between the two. Bankroll studied the plastic stick that contains two pink lines that indicate positive. A small smile began to creep across his face, but quickly dismissed.

Bankroll sat for a minute never taking his eyes off of the test. "Let's get out of here."

Throwing a couple of hundreds on the table, that was clearly way more than the actual bill, then grabbing Jewel by the hand he led her to his car. Headed downtown, Jewel allowed her twenty-eight-inch weave to blow through the sunroof as she rocked her Gucci shades.

There were no words spoken as the two pulled into the Marriott's parking lot. Bankroll leaned over and kissed Jewel on the lips before he exited the car to head inside. Jewel decided to wait in the car so he could handle his business. Fifteen minutes later, Bank sent Jewel a text letting her know their room was finally ready.

Hoping out, Jewel swayed her hips side to side as she met her man in the lobby. Never saying a word to her or barely looking at her, Jewel couldn't help but wonder if even coming to this hotel with him was a good idea.

"This nigga is known to be crazy and his quietness is scaring me," Jewel thought to herself. *"He might just kill my ass right there."*

"Relax baby," Bank said as they entered the elevator. It was like he could feel her nervousness.

Together they rode the elevator all the way to the top floor not saying a word but just holding hands. Once the elevator came to a complete stop, Bankroll instructed her to close her eyes. Jewel could sense when something was off, so she was a little hesitant at first but eventually did what she was told. Bankroll led her off the elevator and led her to the door.

"Don't open them until I tell you."

Jewel nodded her head as Bank removed the room key from his pocket to open the room. Once the door closed, Jewel opened her eyes.

Gasping at the sight in front of her, Jewel was amazed. Candles were lit every inch of the room, rose petals from the door to the bed. She has no idea how he achieved this in fifteen minutes but she didn't give a damn either. There was Champagne on ice with matching robes on the bed. Everything was so beautiful.

"For me?" Jewel asked. Never having a man do this for her she fell straight into Bankroll's arms.

"All for you baby," Bank smiled. "Go ahead and take them clothes off for daddy."

Seductive smile crept across his face as he sat back on the bed. Bank tool lite a cigar ready for the show. Jewel placed her purse on the table by the bathroom. She unzipped her shorts and pulled them down.

"Slower ma," Bank roll instructed. Jewel slowed it down for him. "Leave them heels on."

As she removed her tank top from over her head, her breast sat straight up revealing two perfect pierced nipples.

"Turn around." Bank inhale and exhale the smoke.

With nothing but her heels and thong, Jewel turned around standing confident in her skin. Not knowing what to expect, she had to admit she could feel her stomach in her ass. This was the first time Bankroll ever dragged sex out. Usually she would suck him up, then he would forcefully fuck her to sleep.

Jewel could feel his hand grip her breast from behind as his man hood caressed her back parts. Bank was blessed in so many ways, and he knew it.

Kissing her on her neck, he motioned her hands down to her kitty. Jewel could feel the warmth between her fingers for she was ready to play. There was no doubt that Bankroll turned her on like no other man. Just as he reached to pull her thong down she stopped him.

"Wait! I just want to freshen up for you," Jewel said suddenly.

Taking the hint he backed up and smacked her on the ass. "Hurry yo ass up then."

Jewel grabbed her purse and headed into the bathroom. She closed the door behind her and locked it. Turning the water on, Jewel looked in the mirror as she took five deep breaths. "You got this Jewel."

Placing her purse on the back of the stall as she turned the water off, she opened the door to find Bankroll lying in the middle of the bed with nothing but his boxers on.

Jewel laughed a little as she slipped out of her thong and made her way to the bed. Helping him remove his boxer and straddle him right there. Jewel was ready. Slipping down on his shaft, she rotates her hips to the beat in her head. Their eyes lock.

Starting out slow, she licks her lips in seduction as he massages her breast. Jewel watches as his eyes roll in the back of his head. Knowing she had him right where she wanted him she picked up the pace.

"Right there daddy." Calling him daddy was one of his things. It made Bank feel like he was in control.

"Damn girl who's pussy is this? Bank asked.

"All yours, daddy. Yours!" she screamed.

Jewel focused her attention on her target as she knew he was about to climax. Rubbing her pussy as she rode his dick, she imagined the lavish lifestyle she was about to live due to this pregnancy. As they came together, both collapsing, sweat dripped from Bankroll's forehead.

Jewel could tell there was something different about Bankroll, but she couldn't put her finger on it. Laying there in the moment, he kissed her forehead as he held her in his arms.

Drifting off to sleep, a knock interrupts them. Bankroll was the first to hop up to answer. Never asking who it was like he was expecting someone. Ignoring the visit, Jewel turned over and began to get comfortable again. All she heard was "preciate it" coming from Bankroll.

"Get up!" She felt the cold drift hit her naked body as Bank snatched the covers from her standing there with a bottle of Hennessy and a bag from Walgreens. "Get up and go pee bitch! Now!"

With a confused look on her face Jewel sat straight up in bed. "Bank what the hell?!"

"So you thought you were going to pull a pregnancy test from your purse, and it was all good?" Bank laughed at her stupidity "Get up and piss I don't have all day."

Jewel snatched the Walgreens bag and headed to the bathroom.

"Leave the door open!" Bankroll tone was stern.

Oh this nigga done lost his mind. Jewel thought to herself.

Jewel sat on the toilet with anger. She couldn't believe that he was really making her do this. No matter what this nigga would never take her word for nothing. Bankroll stood in the doorway, watching her closely never taking his eyes off of her.

"Do you really have to watch me, Damn!?" Jewel asked.

"Hell yeah I do. Now piss before I get mad," Bank poured himself a cup of Hennessy as he watched her.

Jewel hung her head and as she thought of ways to make herself urinate on the spot. "I can't go while you're watching, hell I can't go at all."

"Figure it out Jewel!" Bank yelled!

"Can I get some water please?"

Bank reached over to grab one of the mini cups on the bathroom sink and filled it with some water. "Here!"

Jewel grabbed the cup. She couldn't believe she was drinking tap water, but she had to play it cool. She threw the cup down and decided to speed the process up her own way. Placing two fingers over her clit, and she began to rub causing herself to become aroused. Pulling her fingers in and out, her wetness touched her tips. It was like her bladder began filling up by the seconds. Jewel rubbed so more in a fast-circular motion causing Bankroll to become mesmerized with her shenanigans. His dick was hard again, but he continued to stay focused.

"Pass me the test," Jewel order.

Right there, Jewel relieved herself on the stick right in front of him. Placing it on the counter, she wiped herself good and proceeded to wash her hands. Brushing past him back to the bed, she grabs a robe to cover herself.

"Wtf!" Bankroll said

Jewel heart sank. She couldn't really make out his tone, but she hoped for the best. This was her meal ticket.

"Damn ma so you really are pregnant?" He said to her.

Jewel didn't say a word. Bankroll cuddles up next to her and begins pleading his case.

"Damn bae I should've never doubted you. Just believe me I got you forever and two days. Bank said as he rubbed her stomach.

Jewel smiled. Not at the sweet nothing, but at the come up she just finesse. She was glad she decided to leave the vigil of "dummy piss" in her vagina. And it was more of luck that she was able to unscrew the top while she seductively played with herself.

"I love you," Bankroll said.

Never hearing the words from him she sat up and looked over to him. "I love you too daddy."

Chapter 2

Jewel slowly wiggled her body from under Bank's grip. The pair had fallen asleep. Jewel rubbed her eyes as she thought of where she laid her cellphone down. She could see her Gucci bag lit up as the phone continued to ring.

"Hello?" Jewel said.

"You have a collect call from: 'Tati,' an inmate at Alvin S Glenn detention center. Do you accept the charges?"

Jewel's eyes lit up at the sound of one of her best friend's voices.

The two haven't spoken since the night the feds busted Tati from the passenger seat of Juelz car. Jewel didn't have anything against Tati since she's been away, but she made clear to the girls there would be no communication if one was to ever get jammed up by the feds for anything. Including herself. It just wasn't safe.

Rumors were already circulating around, that the girls were tied to a string of date rape robberies involving some of well-known drug dealers. Jewel was unsure what the police knew and thought it was best to cut ties for the time being to conduct business as normal while Tati was away. Only taking dates with some of the richest men in and out of South Carolina, Jewel worked hard to reclaim their image. Catching licks week after week, one at a time making sure they were careful. The fast money was good to them, but Jewel refused to be greedy. Cars, clothes, houses, jewelry you name it. Even though they seem to have it all, Tati wanted more.

It was a Jewel idea to only target the newcomers. The type of niggas who would flash their money every chance they got. The dumb niggas. The ones that lived to impress the crowd. The ones who were blinded by a pretty bitch in need of money.

Every single lick they came out on top. Always enough cash to break off between the three.

Despite business doing good, it was still something missing for Tati. She wasn't happy leaving town every week, sometimes days at time just to eat. With the drug game rising in Dixiana, Tati felt it was enough money here to start hitting licks in their hometown., but Jewel felt different.

Not wanting to jeopardize her relationship with Bankroll and her reputation Jewel was against it. Their career was robbing drug dealers, which included Bankroll, but she just couldn't bring herself to do it. Bank was her ticket out and they all knew it. Tati was convinced that they could complete the lick, with Bank never knowing but Jewel refused.

Juelz was a little nigga from around the way with a decent following. He was an upcoming rapper, only using the drug game to fund his career. Day in and day out he would hit the streets slanging dope up and down 321 highway with his boys. From the looks of it Juelz was definitely getting it.

His brother Juan was known in the streets as well. Only being a year older than Juelz, Juan wanted more for his brother than being a drug dealer. Juelz had pure talent and wanted more for him than just throwing his life away.

It was more to life than fast money and big houses, but it seems like everyone in the hood had the same dream of getting out. Tati couldn't resist the rush, and for that it left her facing some serious charges and her girls out here to fend for themselves.

****

For weeks, Tati had her eyes set on Juelz. His big brother Juan, ran the dirt roads pushing some of the purest Cocaine known to man down in the country. Slangin' dope and heroin to the locals is how he made his living. With both parents lost, to a drug raid, Juan was forced to raise his siblings.

Not many knew that Juan was a silent partner in Beards. He was slowly turning his money clean for he knew this wasn't a life he wanted forever.

"Beards" a perfect little hole in the wall and every Friday and Saturday, it was packed from wall to wall with Dixiana's finest.

"Damn bitch, this man charging fifteen dollars a head for the females," Lena complained.

"And we're not about to pay that either," Tati said as she flipped her twenty-eight inches of weave. "I know Big Ralph at the door. He like a brother to me"

"Everybody is like a brother to you," Jewel said

Jewel was not a big fan of catching a lick on Juelz and Juan. Even though Jewel was all about making a dollar, she was smart. If shit went left, Jewel knew that Juelz and his boys wouldn't think twice about smoking all of them.

"Jewel, get your shit together. We got business to handle," Tati said as she moved closer to the front of the line.

"This ain't the way we do business," Jewel said. We need a better plan. We can't rob this nigga in his own shit."

"Yeah Tati. We didn't really think this through. This is ain't our type of scene," Lena chimed in again.

"Y'all got to learn to trust me," Tati said, trying to reassure them. "Besides, we're not going to rob the nigga in his own shit. I'm take his ass home and you guys follow.

The girls knew there was no way of talking Tati out of her plan. Once everything was a go it was no turning back now. Jewel couldn't believe she let Tati talk her into this. There was an eerie feeling coming over her and Jewel just couldn't shake it.

"Look. just chill. I have a plan. Just follow my lead for once," Tati pleaded.

Jewel nodded even though she hesitated. "Alright fine. But if this shit goes bad, you are on your own."

"Yeah. That's cool with me," Tati answered.

"Everybody got their heat just in case?" Jewel whispered where only them three could hear.

"I'm good," Lena answered.

"Me too," Tati answered next.

All three women had 9mm pistol tape to their dress and Lena carried a pocket knife in her bag for easy access and Lena carried a pocket knife in her clutch for extra security.

"Tati! Tati! Tati! Damn you sho look good tonight girl." Big Ralph greeted his childhood friend.

"Thanks big bro. I see life treating you well" Tati made small talk. *"How's the wife and the kids."*

"Everybody good you know. We're making it. What about you? How is a little man doing?" Big Ralph asked.

"He's good. How much is it tonight?" Tati batted her eyes and poked out her breast trying to get Big Ralph's attention.

Like a man, Big Ralph eye's followed down to Tati's perky double d's. Even though it was a brother and sister relationship for Tati, Big Ralph often lusted over her and she knew it. Using her assets, swayed her body seductively knowing she was being watched. Tati was gorgeous, and her body was tight in all the right places with her caramel skin that was smooth like honey.

"It's fifteen for the ladies and twenty for the guys, but you know I got you." Big Ralph smiled. "How many you got with you?

Tati turned and winked her eye in Jewel direction letting her know everything was good. "Just two."

"That's cool. Go ahead. You know this motherfucker is about to be packed soon." Big Ralph stepped to the side and let the three ladies through.

With Tati leading the way, they enter the club with smirks on their face. Big Ralph didn't even bother to pat anyone down. Each lady knew what they were carrying just in case drama followed them tonight.

"Damn, it's jumpin in here tonight," Lena said as she scanned the club.

"Yeah it is. Let's make sure we stick together," Jewel said.

Making their way to the bar, Tati scanned the club looking for Juan and his crew. She happened to spot Juelz first in the VIP, with bottle girls standing on each side of him.

"Bingo, bitches," Tati said as she turned her attention back to the bar.

The bartender made her way over to greet the ladies. "What can I get you ladies to drink?"

Jewel answered for all three. "Margaritas please."

"And two shots of Hennessy. "Tati added."

Both Jewel and Lena look at her in confusion.

"Who are you ordering shots for?" Lena asked.

"My prey," Tati smiled as she grabbed both shots and her drink and headed toward the VIP.

"Okay look girls remember to stick to the plan. Once we see Tati leave the club with Juelz, then we move. Got it?" Jewel asked.

"Got it." Both responding in unison.

The music was booming from speaker to speaker inside the bar. Dance floor filling up with people, as Tati made her way through the crowd. It was out of any of the ladies element to buy a guy a drink, but Tati needed to. Smoothly Tati was able to slid a roofie, a date rape drug.. In both shot glasses before making it to the VIP.

"Guest only," Juelz's bodyguard steeped in front of Tati causing her to stop in her tracks.

Tati stood there shook for a moment. Looking back toward Lena and Jewel, she could see the "I told you so look" on Jewel's face and she refused to be defeated.

"A list? Boy please I don't need to be on any list. Look at me," Tati took a step back to show off her figure.

Juelz and Juan noticed the noise coming from outside the VIP. "That's fine ass Tati out there," Juelz said as he inhaled his blunt.

"That girl ain't nothing but trouble bro," Juan said.

"Man you say that about all the hoes," Juelz let a laugh. *"Besides, I'm trying to see what kind of trouble she is.*

Juelz watched carefully as Tati and the bodyguard went back and forth. Finally, Juelz whispered to one of his henchmen to tell the bodyguard to let Tati in the VIP.

"Let her in." He said to the guard. *"Juelz wanna see you."*

Tati smiled at the gentlemen then looked back at her girls one last time before slipping inside. Originally she had her eye on Juan, but she quickly noticed how eager Juelz was to let her in. In that moment she decided in her mind that Juelz would be the hit.

Tati smiled seductively as she passed one of the shots to Juelz and took the other one. The both smiled, as Juelz quickly swallowed the liquor. Tati noticed the residue from a white substance on the table in front of her.

"Yo, you into that ma?" Juelz asked.

Tati looked around and noticed other lines lined up ready for the next junkie. "I might be." She said trying to blend in. "But maybe later?"

VIP was crowded with Juelz entourage. A black sectional couch placed in the middle of the floor, was surrounded with beautiful women carrying un-open bottles. The ladies were finishing up their dance and pouring up drinks before leaving the section. Several blunts were in rotation as the gentlemen were living it up. The brothers sat in the middle as they scope the bar.

"I brought a peace offering with me" Tati smiled as she placed the shot in front of Juelz.

"Thanks baby. Why don't come and sit next to me," Juelz flashed a smile showing his mouth filled with Gold.

Tati's pussy instantly got wet at the sight of money in the section. Her heart began to beat fast at *the thought of dollar signs in front of her. Tati knew if everything went as planned, her and her girls would be sitting lovely for the rest of their lives.*

Juelz admired her beauty. As respect, he down both Hennessey shots back to back showing his appreciation to her.

"Just what I needed ma" Juelz said as he placed the empty glasses on the table.

"No problem," Tati said as she slowly sipped her Margarita.

The two managed to talk some more over the music. Juelz showed

o really feeling Tati and her vibe. Tati started to sway her hips to the music, causing Juelz eyes to follow. He pulled her closer to the middle, placing her directly in front of him. Tati moved her hips, as her big ass almost smothering his face.

Burying his ass in her cheeks, Juelz dick began to get hard. The two continued to engage forgetting the VIP was full. Juan dismissed himself and made his way to the bar leaving his brother behind.

"Damn ma. You the truth," Juelz confessed as he stood up behind Tati.

"That's right daddy. I am," Tati whispered in his ear as her body began to heat up.

"I'm in the mood now," Juelz said.

Tati knew the pill was kicking in and it was time. In the matter of time, Tati knew Juelz would be feeling it and wanted to invite her back to his place to continue the party hoping to get some. Once he knocked out, Tati would scope the place out for her, and the girls let them and rob his ass. The plan was perfect.

Easy money, Tati thought.

"You trying to leave with me tonight baby?" Juelz asked.

Tati noticed his words started to slur. She needed to think and think fast. All eyes were determined to be on her if she was to leave with one of the richest men in the building. If Juelz was to show any sign of being drugged, it would be all over.

"Yeah, baby I'm down," Tati agreed.

Juelz signal for one of his men to come over. Each member stood up from their seats to leave. Throwing several one hundred-dollar bills on the table, Juelz led Tati by the hand through the crowd. Jewel and Lena watched eagerly from the bar. That was their cue.

They followed closely behind, as the couple left. Tati used her body weight to give Juelz extra support as he seemed to stumble a little bit, helping him into the driver seat. She figured he didn't live far and could get them there safely. Tati peeked from the rear-view mirror and noticed Jewel's car ready to pull off behind them.

Tati slipped in the passenger side of Juelz's BMW X4, smiling from ear to ear like a little kid in the candy shop. Forgetting she laced Juelz drink, Tati didn't even notice he was the driver.

Heavily intoxicated, Juelz shouted to his crew, pulling off into the night. Blasting his music, Juelz sped down 321 to make it back to the country. Speeding, Juelz looked over to Tati and licked his lips.

"I can't wait to taste you," Juelz admitted.

Tati gave a sly smile and she silently prayed they made it back to his crib in one piece.

Both caught up in the moment, neither of them noticed the black charger pulled out behind them as they turned on Glenn road. Blue and red lights nearly blinded the two.

"Fuck!" Juelz panicked.

Tati watched as Juelz 'movement grew slower and slower. The drug was kicking in, Juelz struggled to stay awake. He managed to pull over to the side of the road, coming to a complete stop.

Tati began to sweat. "Just relax, try not to panic."

"Panic?!" Juelz asked. "I got about maybe two hundred bricks in the trunk right now."

"Oh shit," Tati said. "Just relax. Maybe they won't search the car."

Tati looked over and noticed Juelz in deep slumber.

The pill seems to finally kick all the way in. With the car still running, Tati looked around attempting to plan her escape. Noticing several lights beaming through the back window, moving toward the car. The lights from the flashlight nearly blinded Tati.

"Think, bitch think," Tati said to herself.

The officer knocks on Tati's window with the butt end of the flash light. "Step out the car ma'am."

Tati rolled her eyes as she opened her door. She noticed officer Jonas standing on Juelz 'side of the car. Jonas was known to be a crooked cop, so she knew they were going down. Jonas forcefully opened the driver side of the door and noticed Juelz didn't move.

"Looks like we have a situation here." Jonas laughed. "My type of night. Put in the car and call for backup."

The officer handcuffed Tati and dragged her to the car. Shoving her head in first, he placed her in the back seat before calling for backup. Both officers searched the car, as Tati watched as they pulled bricks after bricks from the trunk, hand guns, scales, weed and bags full of money.

Jonas and his partner laid Juelz flat on the ground as the ambulance arrived.

"Fuck!" Tati screamed.

That night Jewel watched as Tati was arrested. Jonas and his partner seized more than 150 grams of cocaine and crack cocaine. The drugs had a street value of more than fifteen-thousand dollars. Officers also seized nearly two-thousand dollars in cash and four handguns.

It took the feds almost six months to give her a court date. Her son, Max was placed with her mother. As a friend, Jewel made sure Tati books were straight, as well as money for her son. No questions asked. Jewel felt there was no reason for Tati to be calling her.

"Yes," Jewel answered.

She moved quickly but quietly off of the bed into the bathroom. Jewel didn't want to take any chances of Bankroll possibly overhearing her conversation.

"Wow bitch. You really accepted the call?" Tati let out a small laugh.

"Why the hell are you calling me? You know the deal?" Jewel said.

"I don't know shit. Only how you let your best bitch to rot back here while you and Lena continued to live lavishly," Tati tone said it all.

Jewel body began to tense up as she made it inside the bathroom.

"Living lavish?" Jewel voice begin to slightly raise. "The same way you could've been living if you was out here doing stupid shit. And besides I made sure you were more than straight back there. Don't play with me."

"Yeah, well if it wasn't for I wouldn't even be in here," Tati said back

"Bitch you got five seconds before I disconnected the call. I'm not with none of this hot shit," Jewel stood her ground.

"Well if your ass would've showed up for my hearing you would know why I'm calling," Tati said.

"You know I don't do court," Jewel said, growing irritated by the second. She peek through the bathroom door to see Bank still asleep.

"Yeah I know Jewel. Look I'm getting out tomorrow and I need a ride," Tati said getting to the point.

Jewel's heart drop as the words sink in. Never expecting to hear those words from Tati so soon.

"I thought you were at least facing some time."

"I was granted time served. None of that shit matters though. You coming to get me or what?" Tati asked.

Jewel hesitated for a moment. A part of her was excited for her best friend to be back but the other part wasn't too thrilled about possibly having to babysit Tati every move.

Since they were kids it seems like Jewel was always protecting Tati and cleaning up her mess. Jewel was always there when Tati needed her. Growing up in the same hood, the two were thick as thieves. With Jewel being the quieter type and Tati Loud and outgoing.

It was true that opposites attract, for they share equal love for money and hustle. Many times Jewel found herself beating bitches bloody because of Tati's mouth. Tati would pick the fights but could never back her shit up. The duo ran tight together, later bringing Lena in turning the twosome into a threesome.

"Yeah I'll be there to get you," Jewel said. "What time are they releasing you"

"Tomorrow at noon. Bring me a bomb ass outfit too," Tati hung the phone up.

Jewel was fuming at Tati arrogance. There were no plans of Tati getting out this early. Jewel was finally feeling back on top after cleaning up Tati mess from the last mishap. Things were finally looking good for her and Bankroll. She didn't need any more added stress.

In the moment of distress. Jewel quickly finished off the swallow of Hennessy Bank left in his cup on the bathroom counter. "I needed that."

Picking here phone up, Jewel dialed Lena's number.

"Hey Lena, you busy?" Jewel asked her friend.

"No girl. What's up? Why do you sound like that?" Lena asked.

"Nothing girl, I'm headed to your spot in fifteen minutes. We'll talk there."

"Bet," Lena answered.

Jewel hung the phone up and tried to straighten her face up. She did what she could with her hair. Digging through her purse, she pulled out her Mac lipstick to touch it up. Dropping her robe to the floor, she opened the door and was greeted by Bank.

"Who were you on the phone with? And what you gotta talk about in fifteen minutes," Bank asked.

Not knowing how long he had been standing there, Jewel didn't know what to say.

"Oh that was nobody baby but Lena. She went through it with her man and just called me over for some girl talk. That's all," Jewel squeezes her tiny frame by him.

Jewel searched the room for her shorts and tank top. She was trying to make her exit fast before Bank continued with the questioning.

"Girl talk huh?" Bank asked.

"Yeah baby, girl talk," Jewel smiled as she slipped her heels back on.

"That's cool bae. Go do your girl thing and I'll catch up with you later. Here's my keys. Take my car and I'll catch a ride," Bank handed her the keys to his car.

Jewel's eye lit up. She knew she was getting ready to be the talk of the hood. There's been plenty of bitches seen in Bankroll's car, but never in the driver seat. It was beginning to feel official to Jewel.

"Really daddy?" Jewel asked.

"Really baby! And here some money too. Get yourself something to eat later. I need both of my babies to be good and healthy," Bank pulled out a roll of cash.

Jewel took the money and stashed it in her purse and headed for the door.

"No kiss?" Bank asked.

Jewel turned around and leaned in for a quick kiss. "Sorry baby. I'll call you later."

Chapter 3

Jewel pulled up to Lena's house in less than fifteen minutes. Lena was living her best life, in her dream home all by yourself. At the age of twenty-four, Lena owned a five-bedroom house with three and half baths with her and her fur babies Cocoa and Chanel. Business was good for the ladies.

Shortly, after her mom passed, Lena 's dad turned to alcohol to cope with the loss only to lose his life a few years later. He passed due to kidney failure and Lena was left to fend for herself. At the age of sixteen, Lena was sent to live with her grandmother here in South Carolina, but the two never could get along.

Lena would often cry and complain to Jewel how she needed her own space. Living in a two bedroom apartment with four other people would often take a toll on her. With it just being Jewel and her mom, Jewel would allow Lena to stay a few nights put the week causing the two to become like sisters. Night after night, Jewel promised she would have it all and more. Making a way for each of them to see big money by the time they were all twenty. Lena laid low with her money, investing in small business here and there. She was well known for selling human hair bundles and lashes along with dancer outfits for the local strippers. She would stack and save drug money and only buy necessities. Never living above her means.

Jewel parked Bank's car in Lena's drive way and headed toward the front door.. Lena was standing in the doorway with Coca in one hand and Chanel at her feet. Lena's two Pomeranians were like her babies, treating them like children

"Damn bitch. I see you," Lena said, admiring Bankroll's ride.

"Bitch you see me?" Both letting out a laugh as they enter the house. The two friends headed to the kitchen. Lena grabbed a glass from her kitchen shelves and the wine from the fridge.

"I see that little "pee" trick work on his ass," Lena poured a glass of wine.

"And it did," Jewel grabbed the glass and took a sip. "I'll have Bank eating out the palm of my hand before you know it."

"Girl! I'm so glad that shit worked for you". I remember reading that little trick somewhere in a book growing up and I always wonder if it worked," Lena confessed. "Did you seduce him too bitch?"

"You know I did." The ladies laughed.

"I'm so happy it worked out for you," Lena said.

"Well it did bitch," Jewel took another sip noticing Lena never poured herself a glass. "Bitch why are you not drinking?"

"I've already had my one glass for the day," Lena said as she slightly cuffed her stomach.

Jewel placed her glass down on the counter as she studied her friend's movements and demeanor.

Early this week, Jewel reached out for Lena's help, and the two devised the fake pregnancy plan. Never questioning where the stick came from, or the vigil of dummy piss, Jewel was too wrapped up in getting her man.

"Bitch! Say swear?" Jewel eyes lit up and she stared down to Lena's belly.

Since they've been friends Lena has always been the skinny friend, so Jewel knew there wouldn't be a belly, but she couldn't resist rubbing her belly. Jewel was genuinely happy for her, for some reason she knew Lena would be the first mom of the group.

"Thanks girl. These last few weeks have been rough on me," Lena said

"Weeks?" Jewel asked. "How long have you known? We were just turning up in Beardz last week?"

"No bitch you were turning up.' Lena laughed. "I was partying, but I wasn't drinking."

Jewel sat back and thought about how the pair was poppin bottles and throwing cash. Jewel had to admit she was a little smash and not remembering much.

"All those shots that were brought over, you drank by yourself," Lena laughed.

"Damn. I did," Jewel said.

Jewel knew that would be the last week for her to party in the city like that, she didn't want word getting back to the Bank and he started questioning her.

"I didn't want to say anything until I was for sure," Lena said

"I get it. No worries. So, who's the lucky man?" Jewel asked.

Jewel noticed how Lena started to act weird again, but this time it didn't seem Lena really wanted to share the news. Jewel could feel the tension building up, and she couldn't help but think what kind of bullshit Lena was really on.

Lena took a deep breath as she looked her friend in the eye. "Don't trip bitch."

Jewel looked her up and down. "Just say what you need to say."

"Tre's the father."

Jewel stood up from her chair with a disbelief look on her face. "Tre?! Bitch are you crazy?"

"See I knew you were going to trip," Lena said. "It wasn't even like that."

"What do you mean it wasn't like that? You're about to have a whole baby with this man. Hell, do he even know?" Jewel asked.

"He knows and he's excited," Lena said. "He's kinda living here too."

At this point Jewel was stunned. Jewel couldn't believe what she was hearing. "You have officially lost your mind. Why would you allow this nigga to stay here?"

A part of Lena knew Jewel was going to act like this once she found out, but a part of her knew she would be supportive. For so long her and Tre kept the secret, but to be honest Lena was tired of living the double life.

Tre was right up there next to Bank roll with the street numbers. Just as known through the hood as well his pockets were loaded. Jewel was glad Lena was having a baby with a man that could potentially take care of them financially, but Tre wasn't the family type. Barely taking care of Max.

"I thought you would be happy for me," Lena said

"I am happy for you. For baby sake, but everybody knows this man is a dog. He's never going to wife you. Ask Tati," Jewel said.

Tati and Tre were on and off before she caught her case, as well as fathering Max. Tati would sometimes act as if she didn't care who Tre was messing with, but everyone knew how she really felt. Despite the status of their relationship, it was against girl code.

"I don't have to ask her anything," Lena turned her nose up. "I don't owe her anything."

Jewel rolled her eyes. Deep down her heart was telling her, the way Lena was moving was wrong, but Jewel had bigger shit to worry about then some petty bull shit behind a man. Breaking the girl code was minor shit to her big girl problems.

"Well make sure you keep that same energy when the bitch comes home tomorrow," Jewel finished her wine.

Lena stared directly at Jewel as if she saw a ghost. "Tomorrow? I thought her ass was going to do fed time since that old man died."

"You and me both. That's why I was in such a hurry to get to your ass to tell you the news," Jewel said.

"Lucky bitch," Lena grabbed Jewel's empty glass to refill it. Grabbing the fruit try from the counter she made her way to the living room ads Jewel followed.

"Yeah, she always finds a way of getting her ass into shit and out of it," Jewel said as she sat on the couch next to Lena.

"That she does."

"Look girl, I'm truly happy for you if this is what you want. If you see yourself and Tre together then I'm with it, but just watch your back," Jewel grabbed Lena's hand.

"Thanks sis. Means a lot coming from you." They both laughed.

"Another thing, I need you to pick Tati up tomorrow from the jail. She's getting out at noon," Jewel said watching Lena's every move.

"Bitch excuse me?!" Lena jumped straight from the couch. Lena pointed to herself as she paced back and forth. "You want me to go and pick her up?! Bitch are you crazy?"

"Yeah. Why not?" Jewel grabbed a strawberry and dipped it in the yogurt spread. She wasn't fazed one bit about what she was asking.

"Jewel, you have lost it. I just told you less than five minutes ago that her baby daddy is now my baby daddy and you want me to go pick the bitch up from jail tomorrow?!" Lena screamed as she paced back and forth.

Jewel wiped her mouth and then proceeded to pull out her phone. Checking her messages she noticed Bank texted her. A smile crept across her face, as she desperately tried to ignore Lena and the scene she was causing.

"Hello? Do you hear me talking to you?" Lena asked this time with her hands on her hips.

"Well, in my defense I didn't know all of that when I got the call and besides I can't do it. I got shit to do," Jewel wiped her mouth and pulled out her phone. "Besides y'all need to figure that shit out and figure out this baby mama shit ASAP!"

"Jewel I can't."

"What you scared?" Jewel looked up for an answer. "Man tighten up. All you got to do is pick the girl up and drop her ass off."

Lena sat down on the love seat next to the couch. There was no beef between her and Tati. Lena too was there that night, Tati was arrested. It was always hard to tell Tati's mood. Even though., Tati and Tre have been broken up for years, he was still her baby daddy.

"Look I gotta go. I got some stuff I need to handle. I'll text you these details in the morning," Jewel grabbed her bag as she down the last bit of wine. Pulling her Gucci shades from the top of her head to her face, Jewel hugged her friend goodbye.

Chapter 4

Two and a half hours after Jewel left him alone in the hotel, Bank roll decided to hit Siren up for a ride. The two pulled up to the local pantry in the hood, casing the block.

"What was your ass doing all the way on the met, at some fancy ass hotel," Siren asked.

"Nigga you is nosey," Bank said, only half joking.

Siren pulled a two-pack cigar from the middle console. Breaking down the gar and emptying it contents in an empty soda cup, letting the smell of a fresh cigar fill the car following behind the Purp he was about to smoke.

"She must be special if you doing it big like that. I myself take these forty-dollar bitches around here to the motel off of Airport Blvd.," Siren confessed as he licked each side of the gar.

"Yeah nigga I know," Bank laughed.

Siren laughed as he carefully lined his weed inside the cigar. Siren rolled his weed perfectly and used his lighter to dry and seal his masterpiece. Lighting the end of the blunt, Siren inhaled and exhaled as he relaxed his nerves.

"Damn, nigga this all your ass do all day," Bank said as he waved the smoke from his face.

"And you need to start," Siren said, attempting to pass the blunt.

"Nah I'm good. You know I don't smoke that shit," Bank said, turning it down. "Ain't no way I'm be on top smoking my own shit.

"True," Siren said. "So wassup, you had business there or what?"

Bankroll realized Siren wasn't giving up without answers. Siren and Bank were like brothers. Siren was the only Bankroll truly trusted with his life. He figured he told Siren what was up now, before the streets found out.

"I was with Jewel man. She's pregnant with my baby," Bank confessed.

Siren stops in the middle of his puff and stares toward Bankroll. Not saying a word, Siren placed his palm across Bankroll's forehead as if he had fever.

"Come on man I feel fine," Bank pulled back.

"Can't be," Siren shook his head as he outed the blunt.

"What's that supposed to mean?" Bank asked.

"Just when did you start fucking with Jewel like that to get her pregnant," Siren asked.

"That's the thing I wasn't," Bank said. "I mean we fuck around here and there but it was never nothing serious."

Siren sat back in the driver seat. "This is wild man."

"It is man," Bank could no longer contain the excitement in his voice.

"You seem mighty happy about this news," Siren gave Bank a confused look.

"I'm kinda am man," Bank said.

Siren eyes widen. "And you know for sure Jewel is pregnant?"

I made the bitch pee on a stick in front of me and all," Bank said. "I sent one of the hotel workers to grab a test for me."

"You had that girl pee on a stick in front of you man?" Siren asked for clarification.

"On boss I did," Bank chuckled.

"That's some sick shit," Siren laughed

"Shawty hit me up and said she needed to see. We met at Jackson's and she pulled a test out of her purse. I wasn't going for that," Bank said.

"Smart man," Siren said as he dapped Bankroll up. "So what you gonna do now?"

"I'm taking care of me and mine. I never denied the fact that I like the girl, it just always been bad timing. This new baby is showing me I'm right on time now though," Bank said.

"You thinking about wifey her up?" Siren asked.

"I thought about it," Bankroll said. Might as well. Besides, us two together would be unstoppable in these streets.

Siren mood shifted even more. Once he heard the words coming from Bankroll. It has always been them two running the streets of Dixianna together, hearing Bank. talking about doing that someone else made him question their friendship and Jewel's motives.

"I hear ya man. Just be careful. I heard her and her crew ain't no good," Siren said.

"I heard that too, but that's talk," Bankroll said. "Besides, what I look like getting jack by some bitches."

"You right man. That will be a sad day in the hood man," Siren laughed. "I heard her little home girl was really planning on to really rob Juelz the night she went down. I heard she drug the man and all.

Bank sat for a minute as he remembered that night so vividly. Bank was in the club that night popping bottles in the VIP. He watched in silence how Tati seduced her way into Juelz's pocket. He was familiar with Tati but could never catch good vibes from ER. It was Jewel he wanted.

He watched the two leave the club together that night. He expected for his boy Juelz to hit it, break Tati off with a little bit of cash and be done. He never expected to see his boy in a body bag on the news the next day. The autopsy said it was an apparent overdose which caused a heart attack behind the wheel. It was no surprise to Bank on how Juelz died that night. Juelz had been sniffing coke since he got to the club that night. However, there was some speculation that Tati slipped something extra in his drink.

Moments later, Bank noticed Tre's Honda pull up next to Sirens car. Music blasting through the speakers and rims still spinning. Tre flicked his Newport as he exited the car. With   his   jewelry beaming in the sunlight, the glare from his Rolex almost blinded Bank and Siren.

"That nigga act goofy," Siren said.

"Yeah, but he cool people," Bankroll said. "I heard he's getting money."

The two men were familiar with each other but not friends. Tre usually ran solo, only to be a company by females. He believed every man for himself and he stood on that. Occasionally, Bank and Tre would pass each other in passing and keep it cordial. Bank felt Tre attracted to much attention and the wrong attention at that.

Tre made a few serves with the locals before entering the store. Bank noticed a female sitting in Tre's passenger seat on her cell phone.

"That man got a new bitch every week?" Siren said

"That he do," Bank said.

"I heard he was kicking over there with Lena," Siren said. "You know that's supposed to be my girl."

"Nigga please. Lena ain't sweatin you," Bank said.

"Yeah not yet," Siren said, hinting off a little jealousy.

"Yeah never," Bank said.

A few moments later, Jewel pulled up in Bankroll's car with the window slightly down. Bank knew Jewel was flexin' for the bystanders. He found her efforts kinda cute. He knew if the right person sees her in his ride, then the world would know she belongs to him now. That made him smile.

"Look, I'll catch up with you later ," Bank said, dapping Siren up.

"Nigga right now?" Siren asked. He was in mid conversation discussing his love for Lena.

"Yeah man. My baby just pulled up," Bank said, pointing toward his ride with one foot out the car. "Look, if you're admin about getting with Lena, then be just like that man. Every man for himself.

Chapter 5

Jewel and Bankroll made it to his home. Bankroll's garage was attached to the back of the house. Jewel parked the car inside of the garage. The pair enter the house through the side door leading them directly into the kitchen Never seeing the house during the day time, Jewel was taken back at the sight in front of her.

Neatly decorated, the house gave a homey feeling. Bank had workers coming from left and right trying to assist the pair inside.

"Can I take your belongings ma'am?" One lady asked Jewel.

Jewel clutched tight to her bag as she declined the offer.

"It's okay baby," Bank said. "Helga works here."

Jewel relaxed and smiled at Bankroll. Jewel wanted so desperately to impress him, so he would have no problem wifey her. With Bank making it official earlier, she just knew she was in.

"I'm sorry baby I didn't know," Jewel said as she handed her purse to Helga. "Be careful with that. That cost my man a lot of money.

Bankroll laughed as he admired her beauty. Jewel was one the most beautiful women he's ever laid his eye on. His heart skip beats each time he was with her. Her smile could lit up the room. Beautiful long curly hair down her back and smooth caramel skin that glowed in the sunlight. Jewel was perfect to him.

"Bae, why don't you let Helga show you our room. Let here show you around," Bankrolled said.

"Our room?" Jewel questioned as she looked up at him.

Bankroll met her eyes, as his lips followed to her lips with a kiss. Not saying a word, he gazed into

Jewel's eyes telling her everything she needed to know.

Jewel returned gestures as she smiled. Turning to Helga, Jewel nodded that she was ready for her new home. As they walked through room to room, Jewel couldn't help but imagine all the plans she had for this home. Bank's home was filled with eight bedrooms, five baths, indoor basketball court and pool, a built-in home theater and an underground studio. Perfect place to raise a family.

Bank had been proven to own the biggest house in the country. Purchasing the land after hitting his first million, building his dream home from ground up.

"This is the master bedroom." Helga opened two doors and led Jewel inside.

Jewel scanned the room, with her eyes glued to everything. The bedroom was neatly cleaned and was filled with his & hers pieces all over the room. The king size bed placed in the middle of the floor, was covered with black satin sheets. Jewel flopped on the bed as her body stretched, causing the smooth satin to rub against her skin.

"Mr. Chavis requested a full wardrobe in the master closet. Would you like for me to run your bath?" Helga asked.

Jewel sat directly up as if she just won a million dollars from the lottery. "Wardrobe?"

Jewel was overjoyed and felt breathless. Growing up she wasn't poor, but nowhere near rich. Her mother made ends meet never allowing them to go without. Jewel was nothing but a small country girl, with big dreams, determined to live lavish. Having to hustle day in and day out for nice things, she was relieved at how things were looking up for her.

"Yes. right this way." Helga said pointing to the closet area.

Jewel sprinted to the master closet. Clothes from fashion boutiques all around the world caught her eye. Shoes, clothes, jewelry and handbags on display. Jewel even noticed the blue tiffany box wrapped perfectly with bow on the top shelf.

Jewel was tempted to open but decided against, for she didn't want to get her hopes to have her world crushed.

Gracefully, Jewel skimmed through the night wear, setting her eyes on a cute white halter top, with gray plush shorts with matching robe. She rubbed the material against her skin to get a good feel. Kicking off her red bottoms, she slid her foot inside a pair of bedroom shoes.

Helga excused herself after Jewel entered the bathroom. Candles lit each end of the bathroom, with the smell of roses in the air. Soft music playing in the background, as Jewel undressed.

Jewel looked into the mirror, as she pulled her hair up. She admired her body. Turning to the side. She playfully cuffed her belly as if she was pregnant. Swaying side to side, she admired different angles

"Can't wait to see that little bump on you ma." Bank startled her as she entered the bathroom.

"Jesus bae! You scared me," Jewel said, snapping out of her thoughts.

Placing one foot in the bath at time, Jewel tested the temperature. Stepping in with one foot at a time, her white manicured toes glisten under the water. The steam of the bath opened her pours, causing Jewel to relax. Rose petals at the bottom of the tub, added a pure scent of fresh ness.

Bank carefully massaged her shoulders as Jewel laid her head back. "I'm so happy you're here."

"I'm so happy I'm here too," Jewel answered. "I was so glad when you texted me."

During her visit with Lena, Bank sent Jewel a text requesting for her to pick him up and head back to his place for some family time. Jewel was both relieved and happy when she saw the message. She was over listening to Lena's sister wife drama, and just wanted some alone time with Bank.

Bank continued to massage Jewel's shoulders as she rotated her neck in a circular motion. He thought about his feelings for her, and how he was ready to step and take care of his responsibilities. Deep down he loved Jewel, but he could help replaying the concerns he had in his head.

She had proven to him that she was with child, and she would soon have to prove he was the father. Bank knew the time would come for them to have that conversation, but he didn't want to ruin this moment. He wanted to enjoy this journey with her until then. Even with doubts, Bank wasn't going to allow Jewel to go through this alone.

"This feels so good," Jewel said breaking the silence.

"Just relax love, I got you forever," Bank whispered in Jewel's ear causing her to smile.

Jewel leaned up for a kiss. Her soft lips sent a tingle through Bank's body, causing his soldier to stand tall. Placing both hands under her chin, he slowly lifted her up with his lips still attached to her skin. Placing kisses at every inch.

When he reached her breast, his tongue caressed each nipple. Jewel body cringe, as the warmth of his tongue inherits her nipple. His hands slowly rubbed her body until he found her opening. Picking Jewel up, Bank carefully carried and placed her on his counter.

Jewel rotated her hips in a circular motion and his fingers followed. Bank suddenly removed his fingers, as he archived her back toward the bathroom mirror. On his knees, Bank took all of Jewel by mouth. Her legs locked around his neck and Jewel grip her legs tight to make sure he didn't move.

She could hear his soft moans in between her own. She was dying to feel him inside of her, but she didn't want to spoil the moment. She continued to grind against his lips as he played with her clitoris. Jewel instantly had an orgasm causing her body to go weak.

Bank noticed she was defeated, as Jewel's body fell slumped. He picked her up once more, but this time carried her to the bed. He dried her off the best he could and laid her down. Snuggling up next to her, he rubbed her back, sending Jewel in quick slumber.

****

The next morning Jewel woke to a fresh smell coming from the kitchen. Her mouth watered at the thought of the crisp bacon filling her belly. She sat up straight and stretched her body. She'd been overdue for a good night's sleep.

Vision of the night before played through her head as she looked over for Bankroll. She noticed his side of the bed was slightly messed up indicating he slept next to her last night. Jewel smiled as she rubbed his side of the bed. She could smell his cologne on the sheets as if he was near.

Like any curious woman, Jewel began to look at her surroundings. The master bedroom was decorated as a full-blown bachelor's pad.

"I can't wait to decorate this place my way," Jewel thought to herself.

She pulled herself out of bed and grabbed a silk black robe that was placed for her next to the night stand. Her mind wandered at the thought of Bank and where he could be. Just assuming he had business to handle, she figured she would make herself at home. She wanted to freshen herself up before she went down for breakfast. She wanted to look and feel her best at all times for her man

Jewel could hear voices coming from inside the master bathroom. She recognized Bankroll's voice instantly but couldn't make out the other participant he had on speakerphone. She didn't recognize the voice, but that didn't stop her from eased dropping.

"The shipment was supposed to be here two nights ago. We're supposed to meet at the warehouse off old Dunbar road," Bank said in aggressive trying not to raise his voice.

"Yeah I know man. I talked to O'boy and he said Friday." The unknown caller said

"Friday. That's three days from now. I'm losing money from this shit because motherfuckers can't simply handle their business," Bank said.

Jewel moved closer to the door to hear better. She listens closely to the details to the call. She was desperate to know everything about Bank. His livelihood came no surprise to her as she hustled through the small crack of the door.

"I know boss man. I got you. We can't back out now. This a three-hundred thousand-dollar deal on the line. We can't fuck this up now." The caller said.

Jewel eyes widened and her heart skipped a beat as she listened. The bad bitch in her thought about her friends. She thought about just what that type of money could do for them. With that type of money she wouldn't have to scam no nigga with a baby.

"That's exactly why I'm tight about my money," Bankroll confessed. "Look you tell that nigga to be there Friday at midnight. No games."

"I got you, boss." The call ended

Jewel rushed back toward the bed to act as if she just woken up. Deep down she had feelings for Bankroll, but she wasn't in love. It was his pockets that kept her interested and the phone call she just heard confirm everything she needed to know.

Bank entered the room catching her looking for her purse

"Looking for something?" He asked, startling her.

Jewel jumped at the sound of his voice. "I hate when you do that."

Bank was a built guy. This was the first time Jewel really noticed his body frame. She now had to study him since he now became her lick.

"My bad baby," Bank wrapped his arm around her waist to pull her close. "You hungry?"

"You know I am." She smiled back playfully. "We are."

Bank smiled as Jewel rubbed her stomach. He was determined to do right by Jewel. He was tired of the fast laugh chasing hoes. He was ready to settle down and be a family man even if it was with someone like Jewel.

He was fully aware of her reputation but one thing he knew was that she was a hustler just like him. He needed someone like her on his team. To him. Jewel just needed a little guidance and love.

"How about you freshen up and meet me down stairs for some food."

"I would love too," Jewel said smiling

Jewel leaned in for a kiss and he met her half way. Jewel was determined to play her part to get closer to the money. She was willing to do anything he asked. Her only concern was pulling this off alone. Jewel was a tough girl, but she needed her friends for the job. They were a package deal and they completed each other. Each one brought something to the table.

"Okay baby go so I can change." She said playfully pushing Bankroll out of the bedroom."

"Okay I'm going. Don't have me waiting forever Jewel," Bankroll winked at her.

Jewel stood at a standstill as Bankroll left the room. After a few seconds of waiting, she retrieved her cell phone from her purse. Afraid of getting caught, she didn't want to risk being heard, so she decided to send a text to Lena.

"Let me know when you got Tati. WE NEED TO TALK. All three."

-Jewel

Chapter 6

The next day..

Finally, the rain decided to stop pouring. It had been storming all night and the sun decided to come out with a mild rainbow in the sky. Lena arrived at the jailhouse in less than thirty minutes. Tossing and turning all night from the guilt. Lena's eyes were heavy.

It was a little bit after noon, as Lena watched her clock anxiously. Jewel texted Lena yesterday, shortly after leaving her house on where to pick Tati up from. She instructed Lena to pick up Tati a new fit and give her designer bag filled with a little money to hold her over.

She received a text this morning from Jewel, saying they all needed to talk but Lena wasn't in the mood. Lena got up extra early to swing by the mall first then the bank like she was told.

Lena sat and waited for the gates to open. One by one, each newly released inmate flooded outside but no Tati. Lena dug inside her purse for her cellphone to confirm Jewel's instructions, when she heard a loud squeal coming from outside the car.

"Hey bitch!" Tati screamed as she pulled on the car door.

Lena sucked up her pride and hid her emotions well. Forcing a smile on her face, she returned the same energy to Tati. "Oh my gosh! Welcome home girl."

It's been almost two years since Tati was free. Laying eyes on her sent chills down Lena's spine. It seems just like yesterday they were running licks together, and now everything has changed. Tati wearing the dress from the night of the bust, was to be falling off of her. It was evident that she lost some weight.

"Here bitch," Lena threw the Macy bag toward Tati.

Tati slid out of the dress so smoothly. After slipping into a pair of Jimmy Choo jeans and a fitted crop top, Tati let her out of the pony tail allowing it to fall to her shoulders. Tati face was fresh, and her skin seemed to glow.

"Damn girl what they do to you back there?" Lena tried to make small conversation.

"Nothing girl, still the same ol' Tati. I missed you bitches. Where's Jewel?" Tati asked as she looked around.

"She had some business she needed to handle," Lena said.

"Of course she did," Tati said. "It's all good, I'll catch up with my bitch later."

Tati was happy to be free. Feeling like she missed out on so much, she was ready to get back to the money for the sake of her son.

"Here this is for you too," Lena placed a Louis Vuitton bag on Tati's lap that was filled with five bands.

Tati scanned the money as her face frowned up. "Five bands that's it?"

Lena rolled her eyes. "You know the deal. Besides this is just little money to get back in the grove of things."

Tati sucked her teeth but didn't say a word. She knew Lena was right. Besides, there should be nothing out of place as long as Jewel handled her business while Tati was away.

"Yeah alright cool. Tati said stuffing her old clothes into the bag with the money. "So where are we partying tonight?"

"Partying? Girl please is that all you're thinking about?" Lena asked as she scanned Tati for any emotion.

"Girl I've been locked away, with rules, bull shit and more rules. I'm ready to let loose and stack this paper again," Tati confessed.

Lena's face turned up in slight disguise as she watched Tati move as if she was dancing wild in the club. She was surprised that Tati not once asked about her son or Tre.

"I don't know about partying. My business has been doing really well lately and I'm just overly tired. I'm sitting this one out," Lena said.

"Bitch please. That's more than enough reason to celebrate," Tati said.

Lena focused her eyes on the road Merging onto the highway, Lena cell phone ding indicating an incoming call. Quickly looking down, she declined the call before the call connected to the Bluetooth of the car.

"Who calls you trying to dodge?" Tati asked.

"Nobodies," Lena let out a small chuckle.

"Yeah okay," Tati applied some lip gloss she found in the bottom of the Louis Vuitton bag. "Did Jewel give you a cell phone for me?"

"It should be in there," Jewel said never taking her eyes off the road.

"Bet! I need to make a call to my baby daddy and see what's up," Tati stuck her tongue out as she dug through the bag.

Lena's eyes widened as she thought about Tre. Badly, she wanted to pull over and put Tati out, making her walk all the way back to the country she played it cool. Never letting a bitch see her sweat Lena continued to ignore Tati's comments.

Ring. Ring.

After a few more rings, the call went to voicemail. "Damn now this man doesn't want to answer," Tati said as she hung the phone up. "But had no problems answering the collect calls when I was behind the wall..

Lena's heart began to beat at a fast pace rhythm. An unsettling feeling crept across her. Anger filled her soul and she began to see red as she thought about Tati's confession.

"Damn girl. Tre still after you?" Lena asked, making small talk.

"And always will be," Tati smirked as she patted her cat playfully.

Lena's foot pressed the gas causing the car to pick up speed.

"Slow down bitch before you kill us in here," Tati said.

Lena ignored her comments. She was frustrated with the situation at hand. Like a typical nigga, Tre had promised her that he was no longer checking for his baby mama. Lena was having a hard time separating the truth from a lie. Like any woman she was desperate for a one-woman man and she refused to have anything less. She wanted to come clean to her friend right then and there, that she was the new woman in Tre's life, but she knew the timing was off.

Coming to her exit, she wanted nothing more than to drop Tati off, and head straight to Tre's to see what was really going on. Side eyeing Tati, who was just happy to be home again her stomach turned.

"Look, I'll drop you off to your son and meet back up with you and Jewel later," Lena said breaking the silence between them.

"That's cool. I got some business to handle," Tati said.

"Yeah me too," Lena said as she thought about Tre.

She could feel her anxiety getting the best of her as she pulled up in front of Tati's mama house. Her son was playing right in the front yard. He resembles Tre so much that it was scary. The shy little boy stood as he watched the stranger get out of the car. Tati's mother stood on the porch and cried as she barely recognized her daughter.

As they both walked closer to each other, the little boy shyly hid behind his grandmother's leg. He was only three and his mother had been for a little over a year. A bond Tati knew she would have to rebuild. She hugged her mother first, then her son.

Lena watched and became teary eyed at mother's love. She promised herself she would be better to her unborn then her mom was ever to her. She dialed Tre's number, causing him to pick on the first right. Giving him no time to speak she said four words to him …

"I'm on the way."

Chapter 7

"This Friday you said?" Tre asked, as he paced the living room of the trap house as he took his phone call.

Moments later, Lena walked in wearing a white sundress hugging her tiny frame. Her bump was barely noticeable, but yet her glow wasn't invincible. Tre noticed her immediately, throwing his finger up signally for her to give him a minute. Lena spent enough time around to notice he was handling business by his tone.

"Alright bet. Just make sure you check my shit first." Tre said, slamming his flip phone shut.

Lena placed her bag on a table nearby and stuck her designer shades inside. Her insides were fuming, but she decided to play it cool. Even though Tre was the only in her presence. Tre's body was tattooed up and his dreads hung a few inches past his shoulders, with the swag of a street hustler.

"Hey babe." Tre leaned in to kiss Lena on the cheek.

Annoyed, Lena rolled her eyes while placing her hands on her hips. "Don't *hey babe* me. Why didn't you come home last night?"

Tre shot Lena a look of confusion and stopped in his tracks. "That's not my home. You know that."

Tre and Lena have been casually seeing each other for a while now, but Lena wanted more. She wanted a commitment from him. Once Lena found out she was pregnant, Tre showed excitement and started wanting her around more. He would stay a few nights out of the week at her place like a real couple, but she knew in her mind they weren't official.

Lena let out a deep breath. "You know what I mean Tre."

"Do I?" Tre challenged.

Lena took a step back, eyeing him up and down as if she was ready to go toe to toe with an enemy in the street.

"Look I don't have all day. What's up Lena? Something wrong with the baby or something?" Tre questioned her growing annoyed with her presence.

"Nah everything good with my baby," Lena said, cuffing her stomach. "But I did just drop your other baby mama off, and she had a lot of interesting things to say.

"Yeah like what?" Tre asked seemingly unbothered by her comment.

"Like you been fucking with her while she was behind that wall. You taking the bitch calls now Tre," Lena could feel her blood pressure rising and her palms were sweating.

There was no doubt that Lena was in love with Tre and she could stand the thought of another woman getting any of his time. She was to fly to be a side chick and she refused to play that role. Like

Jewel, her gut told her to cut Tre off a long time ago, but her heart wouldn't let her.

"How you sound?" Tre asked. "That's my baby mama. I may have answered a call or two here or there."

"Tre, you said out your mouth you wasn't fucking with her like that no more! Why do you lie to me?" Lena asked, allowing her emotions to get the best of her.

"I didn't lie. I don't fuck with her like that anymore, but she still is the mother of my child. Just like you. Maybe." Tre said, smirking.

Lena's eyes grew wide, for she was furious. Tre was the only man she's been with and he knew that. The thought of him even try to play her like some hoe sent her through the roof.

"Nigga, don't play with me!" Lena said.

"Don't question me." Tre said. "You knew what it was when we started messing around. Besides what's a few phone calls. It ain't like I'm fucking her."

"Yet," Lena said

"Then maybe you need to step your game up."

"I'm not about to compete for you Tre. You need to man up and tell your baby mama what it is," Lena plopped on the brown couch. Next to her it was several Ziploc bags filled with weed.

"Why don't you tell her then." Tre shot back.

He wasn't the type to be a one-woman man, but to him Tati was just his baby mama. He was in no mood to get in between their childish games or to satisfy Lena by telling Tati is every move with a new woman. To him it was no need to prove who he belonged to. In his mind, Tre belonged to the streets and there was no woman alive that could change that.

Lena heart raced, as the thought of facing her former best friend. The way Tati carried on in the car infuriated her. Her stomach was in knots and she was nowhere near excited to tell Tati the truth. Tati was a loose cannon and she didn't want to deal with the drama. Lena simply wanted for her and Tre's relationship to be respected by others even if he didn't. To her she was his Bonnie and she wanted him to be her Clyde.

"I just might, since you can't hold your own." Lena stepped to him.

"Do what you have to do." Tre said, unphased by her toughness.

Tre let out a small chuckled. He knew there was nothing but fear in Lena's heart. She wasn't the muscle of the group, just the pretty one. She was a regular country girl with a sweet personality that wouldn't hurt a fly. He knew she would never have the guts to confront Tati.

"I will," Lena could smell his cologne as it invaded her nostrils. Her pussy muscles thrive as he watches her.

She took a step back from him to catch her breath. She didn't want to give him any ideas. She was in no mood to bust wide open for him after he purposely disrespected her. She had no intentions of caving in, for he needed to be taught a lesson.

"So what was that phone call about? You got some new work?" Lena asked, changing the subject.

Tre turned away from her and continued to count and bag his merchandise up. Lena noticed the money sitting on the table. Within just a few seconds she could tell it was about a little over twenty-thousand dollars sitting right in front of her.

"Yeah something like that." Tre confessed.

"It's a lot of dope in here," Lena said, eyeing the bricks of cocaine sitting in the counter neatly stacked.

Tre looked at Lena, the drugs and then back toward Lena. He was taken back with her interest in his lifestyle. There were time's he would confided in her, but not so much that she could be trusted.

"Yeah it is. I got to move it for some old head from Florida this Friday. Me and Bankroll are supposed to make the exchange. These bricks are worth a lot of money, I can't fuck this up ma." Tre said recounting his paper. He was all nerves.

Tre spent most of his life in the drug game. As a little boy, he watched his father, Big Lou, run the streets from sunup to sun down. Big Lou was a well-known drug lord before his death and had many plugs and connections throughout the South. His biggest connection was a Jamaican a named Sonny, who relocated from Kingston Jamaica to Miami Florida in the late ninties, exporting large quantities of weed and cocaine in the US.

After his father's death, Tre seemingly took over his father's business. Pushing and moving dope throughout Dixianna. He even hook up with some of his father's old connections, including Sonny. He agreed to trap fifteen kilos of Sonny's purest white cocaine and was scheduled to meet with Bank to do the exchange. The two knew each other through passing but never direct business. All he had to do was deliver the coke and Bank deliver the funds. Simple.

Lena listened and watched carefully as dollar signs formed in her eyes. Deep down she wanted nothing more than to turn Tre into a family man and start a new life with her, but a part of her knew they could never be. Her heart wanted love, but her mind was a true hustler. Jewel had taught her the best way to cure a heartache was to get paid

"Let me help with the drop," Lena said, hoping to convenience Tre to let her in.

"Let you help?!" Tre slightly raised his eyebrow toward Lena. "This type of shit is way out your lane ma."

"Come on Tre. I can go with you and make sure everything runs smoothly," Lena suggested. "And I'm sure I can cap any nigga that get out line."

Lena placed her index and middle fingers in a shape of a pistol and pointed toward Tre. Deep down she was serious. Robbing niggas gave her much practice on toting a gun. Tre continued to look at her as he burst out in laughter.

"Ma chill." He chuckled. "You'll be done fuck this whole operation from me. Besides, it's just a drop. Bank is the one moving the work. Not me."

"Tre come on, please," Lena damn near whined.

"Le I said no! Now stop asking damn! I don't need no simple-minded little girl crowding me." Tre said.

Lena took a step back as she was in shock. He had hurt her feelings with his words. Her heart hurt so much for him and he didn't even respect her as a partner. Her insides grew furious as she thought about the life she would never have with Tre as her man. She realized she only had her unborn child and her best friends, and it was time to move on. Her soul was broke, and she wanted revenge. She looked over the room one last time. Placing her designer shades over her eyes to cover the tears that were forming. She grabbed her purse and dash straight to her car without saying goodbye.

Once inside the tears begin to form as she thought about Jewel and Tati. The ladies needed to make things right again in their circle. All this time she was mad at Tati, when Tre was the one you wasn't shit. Digging through her purse she pulled out her phone and responded to the group text Jewel sent out earlier..

Bet. I'm otw.

-Lena

Lena didn't know what Jewel needed to meet about, but she figured she would take this opportunity to present them with a new lick. It was time they showed their hometown that they're not the ones to be played with.

"Best revenge is your paper." She thought as she drove off.

Chapter 8

Jewel was able to convince Bankroll to let her go home for a few hours, so she could gather some of her belongings. He wanted to send someone to box her things up and have them delivered to her. Jewel needed this time to have a talk with her girls and she didn't want to risk anyone in Bankroll's home over hearing her plan.

Lena was the first to arrive. Jewel greeted her friend with a hug before letting her inside. She could tell that Lena was crying but decided not to ask what was wrong at this time. She needed a clear head to focus for business, whatever dream Lena had could wait.

"Wassup girl," Lena said as she plopped down on Jewel's couch. Lena kicked off her shoes as she slouched a little bit.

"Tati should be here any minute then we can really talk," Lena said. "Did you tell her about ol' boy."

Lena rolled her eyes at the mention of Tre. She was so frustrated and was in no mood to discuss him with Jewel or Tati. "No girl. I didn't"

"Well you need to do it soon and make sure she is cool with y'all messing around and having a baby. I don't need no drama in the group right now," Jewel said sternly.

"Yeah your right," Lena agreed. "I'll handle it."

Jewel looked Lena up and down trying to study her body language. "What did he do? "Jewel asked, rolling her eyes.

"Nothing," Lena shrugged her shoulders as nothing was bothering her.

"Bitch stop lying. I know you," Jewel pressed.

Lena sat up to tell her side." I found out that while Tati was away, Tre was still in contact with her. I confronted him about it and pretty much told me there was nothing I could do about it.”

Jewel looked over at her friend with a surprised look. “Okay, and? That’s his baby mama, what did you expect?”

“Are you serious, Jewel? Who’s side are you on?” Lena asked, all of sudden questioning her friendship with Jewel.

“I’m not on nobody's side. I told you I would stay out of it, but you a grown ass woman you knew what it was before you began dealing with him,” Jewel said.

“We're about to have a baby together,” Lena whined.”

“A baby don’t mean shit to these niggas out here but some free pussy time to time,” Jewel said bluntly.

Just as Jewel was about to give her naive friend the rundown, her doorbell rang following a string of knocks.

"Open up bitchesss!" Tati sang on the other side of the door.

Both Jewel and Lena looked over to each other and grew annoyed. It's been a little over a year since Tati's been away and they been able to adjust to life without her loud and obnoxious side. The knocks continued with Tati pressing the doorbell repeatedly. Jewel took deep breaths gathering her thoughts before opening the door.

"Hey girl," Jewel said with a fake smile. Tai through herself into a hug with Jewel.

Jewel could smell the alcohol merging from Tati's body. It smelled as if she was drenched in the liquor from head to toe.

"Have you been drinking bitch?" Jewel asked as she pushed her away.

Tati stumbled in past Jewel to the love seat. The bottle was visible in her purse and her eyes were bloodshot red. Lena rolled her eyes at how sloppy Tati was being.

"Tati I know you are not drinking, and you were just released a few hours ago," Lena asked. "Isn't that part of your probation.

The whole crew knew she had a drinking problem before she did her time. Tati would spend hours getting drunk by herself. She abused alcohol and didn't know when to quit.

"Damn mind y'all business," Tati said, trying to manage her words. "A bitch just got out and I'm trying to celebrate. Y'all need to chill."

"No you need to chill," Jewel closed her door, and walked toward Tati. She snatched the bottle from Tati's purse.

"That's mine!" Tati shot right up now head to head with Jewel.

"And now it's mine. Sit down bitch," Jewel didn't flinch.

Tati took a moment to size Jewel up and down before defeatedly sitting back down on the love seat. Lena shook her head in disbelief. Jewel walked to the kitchen to pour the bottle down the drain.

"What are you looking at and shaking your head for Lena?" Tati asked.

"You!" Lena challenged. "I can't believe you're still on this same bullshit Tati."

"Me? I know you're not talking?" Tati said. She shot Lena a troubling look. "You're the last one to be questioning me about anything."

Lena sat completing still before responding. "What the fuck are you talking about Tati."

Tati stood up pacing the room completely ignoring Lena's question. "Look what are we here for, I got shit to do.

"Answer me!" Lena demanded.

All of a sudden enter back into the room with the empty liquor bottle and a cold-water bottle. "Can you two bitches just chill for two seconds so I can get this meeting over with."

Tati sat back down never making eye contact with Lena. Jewel tossed both the empty bottle and water into Tati's lap as she sat on the couch next to Lena placing her in the middle of them.

"Now let me bring you up to speed Tati. I need you to focus," Jewel said.

"I got you. I am focused," Tati said as she stuffed the bottle in her bag before drinking the water Jewel had given her.

"First I want to say welcome home, we definitely miss you around here," Jewel lied.

"I'm sure you both did," Tati said as she stared in Lena's direction.

Jewel ignored it and continued her statement. "While you've been gone, I've been seeing Bankroll from time to time and I'm kinda like his girl now," Jewel said.

"What you mean kinda," Tati let out a laugh. "Either you is or you ain't"

"I am," Jewel said with confidence. "Not only am I his girl, I'm also carrying his child."

Tati eyes grew wide as she looked at Jewel, then to Lena and back to Jewel. "Bitch say swear."

"Well not really, but that's what he thinks," Jewel said.

"Wait. Wait. Wait I'm confused here," Tati said.

Jewel let out a deep sigh in frustration that she was even revealing this, but she felt Tati needed to know since Lena knew. "I fake a pregnancy test."

"How the fuck do you fake a pregnancy test?" Tati asked, still confused.

Jewel looked at Lena who was sitting in her seat as quiet as a mouse. "I had a pregnant person pee on a stick for me at first and I gave it to him.

Tati laughed again, this time hysterically. "You mean to tell me you gave that man someone else's stick and he believed your shady ass?"

"Not exactly. He made me pee in front of him, so I stuck the dummy piss inside of me and I managed to unscrew the vigil of piss to complete the test," Jewel confessed.

"Wow," Tati said, and she took another sip of water. "Okay, so this is why you called us over here?"

"Lena already knew so no," Jewel said.

Tati eyed Lean once again. "Oh she did? Why wasn't I informed when all of this went down?"

Jewel rolled her eyes. "For one all of this just happened the other day, and two you were locked up. You know the rules."

"Yeah I know the rules," Tati said.

"Like for real what's your damn problem Tati?" Lena asked sick of the antics.

"I don't know you tell me, home girl," Tati said, turning her body to face Lena.

"Why don't you be a real bitch and say what's on your mind," Lena said.

"And why don't you be a real bitch and tell me when my baby little brother or sister is on the way," Tati shot back.

The entire room sat in silence in disbelief. Lena was stuck in between words as she looked to Jewel for help.

"Yeah I know bitch. You think our baby daddy wasn't going to tell me," Tati smirked.

"Look Tati I was going to tell.."

"Save the bull shit for somebody else," Tati through her hand up. "I thought more of you Lena."

"If you knew, why didn't you say anything when I picked you up this morning?" Lena asked.

"And miss a free ride home? Bitch you gotta be kidding me? And besides I was expecting Jewel to be there, not you," Tati said growing irritated even had to explain herself.

"Well it's out now, can we get down to business," Jewel said.

"You knew they was fucking around?" Tati questioned Jewel.

"No I ain't know shit and when she gave me the piss I didn't know it was hers," Jewel said. "I'm just trying to understand why you even care? You was fucking on so many different niggas before you went in. What's the issue?"

Tati gave Jewel a look as she was surprised she was even taking Lena's side. "The issue is Lena is like my best friend and Tre is my son's father. How does that look?"

"Look Tati, I get it. We all know what kind of dude Tre is. We need to focus on this money at hand right now. Leave the sensitive shit at the door, and if it's really pressure we can handle it when all of this is over.

Both ladies knew Jewel was right. Their money and lively hood came first over any nigga any day They needed each other to maintain and Tati needed bands to get back on her feet. Her pride was hurt, but even she knew she needed to put her pride aside to get the job done. Any feelings she had toward Lena; her betrayal would have to wait.

"Okay, so what's the game plan?" Tati asked

"I overheard Bank talking on the phone about a job that needs to be done this coming Friday!" Jewel exclaimed. "Bringing in over a hundred thousand. I say we put our big girl panties on hot this nigga."

Both Tati and Lena looked over to each other in confusion. Neither of them ever expected to hear this coming from Jewel. She was always skeptical about hitting a lick in their city, and now she wanted to rob one of the biggest drug dealers to ever come out of Dixianna.

"Wait a minute, Jewel? Are you sure about this? I thought you was feeling the nigga now you want to rob him in less than two days?" Lena asked.

"I've never been surer in my life," Jewel said. "Besides, I was only feeling him because, I knew he could give me a good life, outside of this chump change we've been collecting"

"What about the baby?" Tati asked sarcastically.

"I'll figure that out when the time comes, but for now I'm going to keep using this baby situation to my advantage," Jewel said.

Neither Tati on Lena said a word. Both sitting straight up at attention getting all of the details from Jewel. Lena couldn't help but two and two together from the information she gathered from Tre earlier today. She was still hurt by the situation and was pleased to hear what type of move Jewel was on.

"Only thing this will not be like our regular stick ups," Jewel continued. "Instead jacking these niggas for the paper in their pockets, we're going for the whole thing."

Tati's eyes lit up. "What do you mean the whole thing?"

"We're gonna rob Bank right before the drop," Jewel said with excitement in her eyes.

"Yeah how the fuck we gone do that?" Tati asked. She started to feel Jewel was in over her head.

"Easy," Lena chimed in. "We have inside coming from both parties."

Jewel looked over to Tati as Tati stared Lena down. "What are you talking about Le?

Lena put her head down for a minute as she thought carefully about her next words. "Look, the same drop you over hard Bank talking about this morning is the same drop Tre told me about right before I came here.”

Jewel shot up from her chair and jumped in excitement. The plan was coming together so smoothly for them and she was loving every minute of it.

“What do you mean he told you about it?” Tati questioned sounding a little jealous in her tone. Tre had never shared any of his business moves with her while they were dating.

Lena rolled her eyes as she caught Tati's tone. “He told me about it. He told me the drugs came from a Jamaican cat named Sonny who lived in Florida. He hired Tre to move the bricks. Bankroll is the buyer.”

“Lena this is perfect!” Jewel exclaimed. “You got to get him to tell you more.”

Lena sat back on the couch and took a deep breath. “That's the hard part I don’t know about Jewel. He talked a little bit but when I pressed him about tagging along before I knew your plan he wasn't with it."

Jewel placed her hands on top of her as she rubbed them through her hair. "Think, Jewel think."

Tati let out a little laugh as she watched her friends stress over the idea. "You bitches really trip me out."

"Oh yeah what's your big idea?" Lena asked, challenging her.

"All you gotta do is use what you got to get what you want," Tati stated.

"Oh lord, here this girl goes, using movie quotes and shit," Jewel through her hands in the air dismissing Tati,

"No for real. Here me out. Since you are already the closest thing in this room to my baby daddy, keep pressing him. Make him trust you. He'll be speaking before you know it.

"How am I supposed to get information in two days?" Lena asked.

"Use your imagination," Tati said.

"She's right," Jewel spoke up. "We both got to."

"It's just too soon J," Lena said.

All the girls knew this was risky. They couldn't help but feel that they may be in over their heads, but deep down they all knew this would be their biggest payday.

"We just have to move smart," Jewel said. "You work on Tre and I'll work on Bank. We'll meet back here early Friday morning. Cool?

Yeah cool," Tati said.

Lena just silently shook her head that she understood.

Chapter 9

Tati stood in front of her house, where her mother had been living with her son for the past year. When Tati was jammed up, cps temporarily placed the boy with her mother while she did her time. Tati was thankful to have a place to return to, but her house was nothing compared to Jewel's and Lena.

Them bitches really making moves without me, she thought to herself as she took a pull of her Newport, a nasty habit she seemed to pick up during her time away.

She took a few more puffs and flick the cigarette as she walked up the door steps. She could hear her toddler crying from the outside and her mother scrambling to cater to his every need. She slipped inside quietly as she placed her purse next to the doorway.

"Tatianna is that you?" her mother called out.

"Yes ma. It's me," Tati answered hoping that her mother didn't hear her.

"Girl, I told you I had something to do, and the first thing you do is to slip off somewhere." Her mother said, placing her son in her arms.

"Ma, I had to meet Jewel and Lena for a quick second," Tati pleaded.

"Yeah, yeah. You're gonna get enough of meeting up with those girls. They don't mean you know good Tatianna." Her mother continued. "Especially that Jewel girl."

Tati rolled her eyes at her mother's words and made her way into the living room. She placed her son in the play pin in front of the T.V. She plopped on the couch and flipped through the channels. Her mind was weighing heavy since her talk with the ladies. She was still hung up on the thought of Tre and Lena having a baby, fake pregnancies and Jewel itching to rob Bankroll. It was all too much for someone who just got home yesterday.

She noticed her son begin to settle down as the T.V. seem to catch his attention. Just wanting to take a nap, Tati stretched her legs on the couch and closed her eyes. She could still hear her mother mumbling from the kitchen causing her not to be able to relax.

Irritated, Tati jumped from the couch to retrieve her purse. She scrambled through quickly to pull out a little baggie that contained a little white substance.

"Bingo," Tati said as she admired the prize.

On her way home, she ran into one of the big homies at the corner store who recognized her. He felt bad for not having anything to offer her as a welcome home gift, that he pulled out the small baggie and handed it to her. She only tried the drug a few times while behind bars but loved the feeling it gave it. It relaxed her.

Hurrying back to the living room, she grabbed a book and emptied the substance quickly using her pinky finger to create the perfect line. She used an old receipt paper to create a straw like figure to snort.

Taking the first hit, Tati placed the straw to her right nostril and snorted the drug. The blow sent her adrenaline into overdrive. Placing her head back, she allowed all of her problems to swift away for the moment. Tati placed the straw in the left nostril and repeated.

After she was done she carefully slid the book under the couch to hide the evidence. Tati was high out of her mind and all of her worries seemed to fade away and she attempted to lay back down.

Just as she was about to drift off to sleep, the power in the home shut completely off causing her mother to curse and her son to scream.

"Yo what the fuck!" Tati screamed as she tried to cut the T.V. on with the remote.

Next she tried the light switch flicking it on and off several times with no luck. "Fuck! Mama did you pay the bill?"

Her mother came flying into the room in a rage Tati never seen before. "With what money Tati?!"

Tati looked in confusion as she turned the flashlight on from her cellphone. "The money Jewel is supposed to give you to maintain."

Her mother sucked her teeth so hard as her body filled with anger. "Girl please. That girl has barely been by here since you were gone. She ain't never help me."

Tati knew her mother was on social security barely making enough to put food on the table. It was agreed that Jewel would take care of things while Tati was away and that included Tati's bill.

"Ma what are you trying to say?" Tati asked, growing irritated.

"What I'm trying to say is, Jewel ain't did shit for us." Her mother said. She walked over to the coffee table where a stack of mail laid. She picked up the pile and placed it in Tati hands showing her just what was owed.

Tati skimmed through the stack of mail and noticed one important to document. It was a letter from her mortgage company stating that she had paid a house payment in the last six months and would need to evacuate in the next thirty days. Tati's eyes filled with tears, but she didn't let them drop.

Her body was trembling from the anger she felt. Her best friend allowed her house to foreclosure where her son lived. She couldn't believe what she was reading. Two of the people that she trusted the most let her down and she had nowhere to turn.

Tati knew she had to think and think fast. She didn't want to risk saving her son taken, and her and mother being homeless. She quickly fixed her face and checked the time on her cell.

"Ma I need you keys," Tati said.

"What? Where are you going at a time like this?" Her mother asked.

"I got everything under control. You just stay put and the lights should be back on in about an hour," Tati said, grabbing the keys from her mother's hand.

Tati stuffed the mail in her purse and rushed out the door. She still had the little bit of money Jewel had given her. She needed to make it to the place to pay her bill to get the electricity back on for the night, and she would work on her bigger problem in the morning.

****

****

Later that night Tati made her way down to five points to enjoy some drinks. She decided to go alone. Tati felt she couldn't trust anyone and needed to get her head together. She managed to make it down to the building to pay her bill to get her lights back on. The thought of it made her piss. She contemplated on how to confront Jewel, but she decided against it. Their time was near.

Sitting at the bar, Tati wore a slim fitting pink dress with no straps that hugged her curves. She ordered another shot of Patron and a margarita to get her night going. She skimmed the bar as she noticed it wasn't crowded at all.

"Can I get you another?" The bartender asked.

Tati looked down as she noticed her margarita was more than halfway gone. "Yeah that's fine."

Tati took the shot of Patron before sliding the shot glass back to the bartender. A group of guys entered the bar together. She instantly recognizes Juan amongst the crew. Engaged in deep conversation with someone who Tati wasn't too familiar with, they headed to the back of the bar to grab a table away from everyone.

"Fuck!" Tati thought to herself. This was her first-time seeing Juan since the incident with his brother last and she didn't know how he would react to seeing her.

Tati continued to scope the scene as more people continued to come in, She figured she would order one more drink then head home. The lights inside the bar were dim. Siren and Juan continued to chop it up. Both men each had a bodyguard standing next to them.

"I wonder wtf these to niggas talking about," Tati said to herself.

She reached into her purse and threw some money onto the bar table to cover her bill. She grabbed her drink and walked toward the ladies room in the bank of the bar. She swayed her hips back and forth just in case anyone was watching her as she made her way through. Her eyes met Siren's just before she entered the bathroom.

Tati peaked under each stall to make sure the stall was clear. She dug inside her purse and pulled out a small compact mirror. Inside contained another bag full of pure white cocaine. Tati spread the powder the best she could across her little mirror and took the hit. With her heart racing inside of her dress, Tati smiled as the drugs kicked in.

She used the small mirror to check the details of her nose. She wiped off the excess powder off her nose and closed the mirror. She checked her hair and outfit in the mirror to make sure she was still well put together.

Once she was finished she washed her hands, before leaving the bathroom. Tati stepped outside the bathroom and looked around. She watched as Juan and Siren dap each other before Juan left the bar. She hiked her dress up just a little more to expose her thighs before walking past Siren's table. This time walking a little closer.

"Yo don't I know you?"

Tati stopped in her tracks and smirked. "I'm sorry?" Tati said, acting as if she didn't know him.

"Don't I know you?' Siren asked again. "You look mad familiar."

"I don't know do you?" Tati asked. She was high and feeling herself.

"Yeah I believe I do," Siren said. "I just can't put my finger on it."

Tati slightly rolled her eyes at his effort to flirt. She knew in the back of her head they never met, but she couldn't help but feel she may have seen him somewhere before as well. Still in her feelings from earlier, she just wanted to have some fun to keep her mind clear and off of Jewel and Lena

"Yeah you look familiar too," Tati responded.

"Well I would like to get to know you if that's cool," Siren said, letting out a small laugh. "I'm Siren."

"Tati."

Tati was a little turned off by his pick-up lines. In her mind, they were whack, but the gold Rolex on his wrist along with the gold chains around his neck told her, this cat had money. That was good enough for her.

"Why don't sit down and have a drink with me? So, we can talk," Siren said as he snapped his finger signally for his men to order him another round.

Tati sat down where Juan originally sat and placed her hand bag on the table. Siren took a moment to observe her. He smiled as their eyes connected.

"You from Dixianna right?" Siren asked, making small talk.

"Yeah I am," Tati answered. Her palms begin to sweat as if she was nervous for some reason.

"Well I'm still kind of new around here," Siren admitted.

"Oh really?" Tati asked. "How do you figure you've seen me around before then?"

Siren's worker returned with the drink and he took a sip. He placed the glass on the table and placed both of his on the table as he sat up to face Tati.

"I moved up here about a year ago, from Florida after my little cousin Juelz died from a supposed overdose. I was in town visiting that weekend in the club popping bottles and what not. I ended up linking with a nigga named Bankroll," Siren said.

Tati's eyes widened at the mention of Juelz's name. She thought back to that night to see if she could place his face, but she couldn't. She wondered if he knew she was with him in the car that night. So many thoughts were running through her head and she could feel her anxiety getting the best of her. She regretted giving this nigga her real name now, as she constantly looked over her shoulder toward the exit plotting her escape.

"I'm not sure if you noticed the guy I was talking a few minutes ago, but that's his brother," Siren continued interrupting her thoughts.

"No I didn't. Sorry," Tati lied.

"Yeah, but enough about me. If you're from here, how come I never saw you around here in the last year," Siren asked.

"I've been out of the country," Tati lied again.

"Is that right? So you like to travel ma?" Siren asked.

"Yeah I do."

That's cool to me. I have plans to travel to Jamaica to visit some family I never met, but I gotta handle some business first," Siren said.

Tati listened as Siren talked about himself more and more. She was having a hard time focusing with her mind everywhere. All she could think about was the betrayal her friends had caused. She didn't want to believe the two main people she loved deeply could ever cross her, but she was wrong.

"You want to get out of here?" Tati asked, interrupting Siren.

Siren looked her up and down before he spoke. "Sure thing ma."

Siren pulled out some cash and handed it to his worker to go pay the bill, before downing the rest of his drink. "Where to?"

Can we go back to your place?" Tati asked in a seductive whisper.

Siren's eyes lit up because he realized what type of game she was on. Tati was a party girl and he could tell. She thought she was beautiful, but he can tell she had a long night and just wanted to spend some more time to possibly get to know her.

"Yeah we can do that," Siren stood up and pulled out Tati's chair.

Tati stood up and locked arms with her date and headed out the bar. Siren's car pulled up to the sidewalk, and they both slid in the back. They both sat quietly the entire ride. With Siren sitting close to her, he managed to slide his hand onto Tati's thigh causing her body to be alarmed.

Tati looked into his eyes and was ready to match his energy…. for a small cost.

Chapter 10

Jewel laid in Bankroll's arm on his couch, as they watched Boyz in the hood together. BET was now playing this movie every day of the week it seemed. She snuggled up to his as his cologne filled her nose causing her pearl to tingle in between her legs.

Jewel often found herself confused about her feelings for him. On the outside, Bankroll just seemed like another street dealer with a fuck boy attitude but on the inside he was every girl's dream. A provider.

Jewel spent the last few days getting to know him, as he showed her what a man should be. The thought hurt her a little bit, knowing in the end she would have to double cross him for a better life. Even though Bankroll was expecting a baby from her,

Jewel was no fool and she knew no baby would never keep a man around. Besides, she wanted more to life than to be a dope boy's baby mama. She had to think of herself first.

"Do you want something to drink baby?" She asked sitting up facing him.

"No I'm good baby you?" He asked.

"Yeah a little. I'm going into the kitchen to fix something and I'll be right back."

"Chill bae and relax. I got someone to do that for us. You don't have to move a muscle for anything anymore," Bankroll was serious as he looked into Jewel's eyes.

"Yeah I know baby but let me do my wifely duties." She said jokes. "I need to get used to it; don't you think?"

"No wife of mine will ever be my servant," Bankroll kissed Jewel's lips softly

Jewel smiled at the gesture. She so desperately wanted to get to the kitchen just to check her phone to see if it was any update on their little operation. In a matter of days Jewel will be long gone living her best life with someone's else's money.

"You're too good to me," Jewel said. "I'll be right back.

Jewel quickly got up as she made her way to the kitchen. She grabbed a glass from the cabinets and fixed herself a glass of water. She pulled her phone from her breast and typed a text to Lena.

"Any update?"

She noticed the gray bubbles forming at the bottom of the screen noticing that Lena was in the mist of responding. She took a sip of water and waited. Her phone dinged letting her know there was a response.

"No."

Jewel sucked her teeth in frustration and typed a text back.

"Keep trying Le."

Jewel stuffed the phone in her bra and grabbed the glass and headed back to the living room to join Bank. He was on his phone typing out a message. She tried her hardest to read the message without being noticed, but he closed the messages once he realized she was back in the room.

"Miss you girl." He said playfully and he kissed her on the cheek.

"Miss you too," Jewel said back as she got comfortable again in his arms. "Who was that?"

Bankroll hesitated for a moment as he was taken back at the fact that she was even questioning him.

"Oh that was nobody bae. Just Siren telling me he met a little freak at the bar and was taking her home," Bankroll said.

"Oh wow," Jewel said.

She couldn't even imagine who would even want to be in Siren's company. It was no doubt in her mind that he was getting money, but he was just so lame to her. He moved her about a year ago right around the time Tati got locked up and has been in Bankroll's shadow ever since.

"Yeah I was telling dude to be safe," Bankroll said tucking his phone back into his pocket. "I'm glad someone caught his attention so he can stay out of my business.

"What do you mean in your business?" Jewel asked.

"Nothing man. He was just a little concern about you and I? Bankroll said.

Jewel rolled her eyes as she thought of how Siren may be a problem. He looked like the type to mind everyone's business but his own. She made a mental note to herself to figure his game out before it was too late, before he figured her out.

"Yeah he needs to worry about himself," Jewel added.

"Relax baby. I got to handle it," Bankroll said as he hugged her tight.

****

****

Lena walked around her house in just a black lace thong and in some high heels. She buried her pride and invited Tre over for the night sending him messages back to back on how she was tripping. She vowed to stick to plan and to get as much information as possible so they could pull the job off.

Standing in her kitchen Lena poured Tre a glass of Hennessy. She closed her phone after reading a message from Jewel and headed back up the stairs to the bed room. Setting the mood the right, Lena played slow jams on her Alexa and had candles lit every inch of the room. Tre laid in the middle of the bed smoking a blunt. He inhales then exhales the weed smoke causing his mind to relax.

"There goes my baby." Tre said as Lena entered the room.

Handing him the drink, Lena smiled as she greeted him "Here you go daddy."

Tre sat up, as Lena crept behind him to massage his shoulders. His tight muscles tense up as her soft hands rub his body. Tre spent some time locked up a few years ago, where he worked out daily.

"Just relax baby. I'm put on you tonight," Lena whispered in his ear.

"Yes baby I am." Tre said.

Taking one last puff, he put the blunt out on Lena's night stand. He flipped her over with the quickness. Using both of his he slipped her thong off causing her kitty to stare at her in the face. Lena took a deep breath as Tre began to kiss the inside of her thighs.

Tre had a way of teasing her every single time they had sex. Lena grip the sheets as she anticipates the dick. Heart was full and she loved Tre. Her body was submissive to him and he knew it.

Without warning, Tre took all of her into his mouth and Lena rotated her hips to the song that was playing in the background. She closed her eyes as she imagined the life her and Tre could have together. The King and Queen of Dixianna. The thought caused her to climax before she knew it.

Tre gently flipped her body over, putting her in the doggy style position. Lena's arch was perfect as she poke her ass in the air and spread her legs waiting for him to enter her from behind. Her juices flowed down her leg sending over the edge. Tre jammed his manhood inside of her and began pounding, causing Lena's Double D's to bounce up and down.

Lena let a scream as Tre pulled her hair causing her head to fall backwards. Ever since she been hooking up with Tre he introduced her to rough sex, and she loved. He cuffed her neck, almost suffocating her.

"Yes daddy right there," Lena screamed

"You love daddy?" Tre asked, hyping her up.

"Yeah I love daddy," Lena said in between strokes.

Tre smacked her ass and she let out a moan causing his dick to pre cum just a little."

"Come on nut for daddy." He instructed.

Lena knew she wasn't. She buried her face in the pillows as she threw her ass back like a pro causing Tre to throw his hands in the air. Tre head fell back ready to release himself inside of her. He gripped her hips as he sped his strokes up. Lena lips grip around his tool, as he let himself go inside of her causing both of them to collapse at the same time.

"Damn that was good." Tre said painting.

Lena just smiled as she looked over to him. She stared at him helplessly and she thought about her actions. Tre hoped and made his way to the bathroom Lena heard the water run for a minute and she assumed he was just cleaning himself up. Lena noticed his phone on the night stand. Lena looked to see if Tre was coming before she grabbed the phone and to her surprise there was no lock on the phone.

"Idiot," Lena thought to herself

Lena swiped the phone up causing it to open. Lena searched through the phone looking for any evidence that would help them with the lick. Her heart raced as she was able to attach Bank's name to the messages.

"Got him!" Lena whispered.

"Yo what the fuck are you doing?" Tre said, startling Lena.

Lena was caught red handed. Her palms were sweating uncontrollably, and her heart started to beat faster as she turned and faced him.

"Are you deaf bitch?" Tre asked. "Why are you in my phone?"

"I was.. I was just.," Lena stuttered. She couldn't seem to find the words and her lies weren't coming fast enough.

"You were what?" Tre snatched the phone from her hand. "You're still on this Tati shit I see."

Lena looked confused for a minute before she realized that he thought she would be looking through his phone for the scoop on his baby mama. She decided to play along.

"Yeah I guess I was," Lena said as she folded her arms.

"Look, I ain't with all this checking up on. You either gonna play your part or keep it pushing." Tre said with a serious tone.

"Boy whatever," Lena said as she got up and went into her bathroom next. She was able to remember the address and needed to write it down quickly. She spotted her lip liner and grabbed a piece of toilet paper as she wrote down the information. She smiled at her accomplishment, but she knew she needed more.

Lena flushed the toilet and ran the sink water to make it seem she went in there for different reasoning. She could still hear Tre mumbling under his breath. Returning to the room, she grabbed her robe to cover herself. She looked over to Tre fully dressing himself.

"Going somewhere?" Lena asked.

"I got to make a play." Tre said, never looking at her.

"I thought you were going to stay." She asked. Lena didn't really care if he stayed or went but she wanted to see if she could get any more information out of him.

"Nah you on some other shit tonight, and besides money calling. I'm sure you saw that when you went through my phone." Tre said.

"Well, are you coming back?" Lena asked.

"What's with all the questions? I'll see you around." Tre said as he slipped on his jacket and headed out the bedroom door.

Lena followed behind him hot on his trail. She knew she pissed him off, so she chose her next words very carefully.

"Tre I was thinking about that big drop you were telling me about earlier, and I still think I could help you out a little bit," Lena said boldly.

"Lena, I have told you no already. Leave it alone." Tre said.

"I know. I know but what if I know something already about it besides the stuff you told me," Lena said.

"Tre stopped in his tracks and turned to face her. "Like what?"

Well you know Jewel is kicking it with Bank now, and I remember you telling me he was your buyer right. Well Jewel told me last week that Bank was looking to actually rob you for the drugs and keep the money for himself," Lena lied

Tre crossed his arm revealing his muscles. His eyebrows rose in anger as his bottom lip tightened. "How I know you not bull shitten me Lena?"

"He told Jewel his plan and arranged for her to meet him down the street after the hit so they could go away together.."

Tre was silent. He couldn't believe the news he was hearing. He knew Bankroll from around the way, and never had a problem, but they weren't the best of friends. Which gave him all the reason not to trust him.

"I appreciate you." Tre said as he leaned to kiss Lena on the cheek before heading out the door.

****

****

Siren and Tati pulled up to his place in less than twenty minute. Tati was eager to move their encounter from the car to inside the house. The small hit of coke from earlier was now sending a rush through her body causing her to feel aroused. The entire ride, Tati could feel her body taking over her mind as her juices drip from her honey pot.

She placed Siren's hands in between her thighs, allowing her to feel her warmth. She noticed the bulge in his pants letting her know he was ready to go. He gripped her breast and sucked on her neck using his free hand to caress her back.

"I can't wait to feel this shit ma," Siren confessed.

Picking a woman up from the club was so out of his character, but he was feeling Tati. The way she carried herself was exotic to him and he was well turned on.

"Let's go inside baby," Tati whispered in Siren's ear.

The two hopped out the car and headed to the door. Siren's house spoke volumes on just how good he was doing in life. He lived in a quiet gated community. Tati eyes formed big and she looked over the outside. She only remembered seeing houses this big on the tv screens of rich and famous people.

"This mothafucker got money," Tati thought to herself.

Siren placed the key in the lock and held his finger up signing to give him one second. He slipped inside the door to disable the alarm. Tati stood on the outside of the door slightly annoyed. She knew she didn't know him well and there was no reason for him to trust her this early with the alarm code to his house.

Once the alarm stopped, Siren opened the door and reached out for hers. Tati grabbed his hand and stepped inside the house. Tati eye's grew even bigger at the sight of the inside and how beautiful it was decorated. The house seemed to have a woman's touch, but Tati decided against making it an issue out of her thoughts.

Reading her mind, Siren shut the door behind her and said., "My mother did a good job decorating and giving it a woman's touch."

Tati laughed because she felt foolish. "Yeah she did."

Siren poured himself a glass of scotch and handed Tati a shot glass full of Hennessy. The both drank the contents and Tati held her glass out for another. Siren poured Tati another shot and watched as she down the liquor.

"Damn girl," Siren laughed.

Tati placed the glass down and started kissing Siren aggressively. She tugged at his shirt until she ripped it off his tightly ripped muscles exposing a wife beater underneath. Tati continued through each layer of clothing until Sire's bare chest was exposed. His body was ripped perfectly with the perfect dip between his abs and his pelvic bone,

Tati's mouth water as she pressed her body against his and slowly caressed his man hood through his pants. She licked his ear sending a chill through his spine causing his hand to find his way to her honey pot once again. Siren could feel his fingers dripping wet from her moist.

In his mind he wanted to take Tati right there on the floor, but he wanted to do it right. Siren grabbed her hand and led her up the stairs into the master bedroom. Tati's head was slightly spinning, and she wanted to lay down, but she maintained her composer as she held a tight grip to Siren's hand. As they entered the room, two large pit bulls began to bark viciously at the pair.

"Yo what the fuck?!" Tati screamed, as she jumped back.

Siren let out a small laugh. "Yo relax. These are my babies. You good."

"I'm good?! These motherfuckers bite," Tati said.

"As long as you're with me, you're good with them. They will only attack if I tell them too," Siren confessed.

Tati's heart pounded and breathing became irregular at the sight of the two large dogs sitting in front of her. Their mouths watered as they stared Tati down. Their tails seem to wag at the same beat as Tati's heart waiting to attack.

"Why are they so damn big?" Tati questioned as she eased inside the door.

Siren walked toward the dogs, petting each one to calm their spirit. "Cause I feed them good," Siren said sarcastically as he eyed Tat's every move

Tati rolled her eyes. "I can tell."

After a few minutes, Chico and Loc both laid silently on the floor and seemed to calm down. Tati was fearless but growing up in the hood she knew better to fuck with two hungry Pitbulls. She tried so hard to relax her mind and body and she knew her high was gone.

"You got anything we can smoke?" Tati asked.

"I don't smoke like that shit ma," Siren confessed. "It's bad for business."

Tati rolled her eyes. "Well do you have anything I can smoke?"

Siren walked over to the night stand and pulled out an electric Vape Pen that contained THC. Tati discretely consumed the marijuana into her lungs to feel a high. She blew the smoke from her nostrils and her body settled.

After a few more puffs, she handed it back to Siren and began to slip out of her dress. She stood confidently in front of Siren exposing her bare-naked body. Her nipples grew hard as she eyed Siren. His mouth water as he removed his clothing and his man hood stood at attention.

"You ready?" Siren asked as he stroked his manhood.

Like a shy girl, Tati shook her head yes as she laid back quietly on the bed. Slowly Siren crawled on top of her, to position himself inside.

****

****

A few hours later, Tati laid on her back staring up at the ceiling. She was unable to move, for her small frame was pinned under a 260-pound Siren. Once they made it back to his place the pair smoked and took ecstasy pills all night, causing Tati not to remember much. Siren passed out on top of her after the two-finish having sex. He snored loudly in her ear, keeping Tati awake.

Tati tried to push Siren off of her, but she failed. She desperately wanted to sneak out and make it home to her son before the sun came up.

"I got to get this nigga off me," Tati whispered.

She could feel Siren move his body a little bit to reposition himself, giving Tati enough room wiggle free. Allowing her eyes to adjust to the dark room, she quickly searched the dark room for her dress and purse. She spotted her heels across the room next to the pants Siren took off earlier. She tiptoed quietly to retrieve them and noticed a stack of money falling out of Siren's pockets. Her first mind was to grab the money and run but she didn't want to risk setting the dogs alert. Deep down she was too weak for a fight and just wanted to get home.

"You leaving me ma?" She heard a sleepy Siren asked."

Tati rolled her eyes. Her body cringed at the thought of him waking up. "I gotta get home to my son. It's late," Tati lied.

Siren sat up in the bed. "Your right. It is late and I'm sure he's fine. Why don't you get back in the bed and I'll take you home in the morning.

Tati looked over to the door as the room spun. She thought the high had warned off, but her body was still numb as if she just inhaled the drug. Her mind was in such a daze that the door seemed further away. Her legs were weak, and she could feel them shake at each attempt she made to move.

"I really should go Siren," Tati pleaded.

Tears formed her eyes. Her stomach felt nauseous causing a dizzy feeling. She leaned against his dresser trying to hold herself so she wouldn't pass out. Siren Sprinted from the bed just in time to catch her fall. He carried her to the bed to lie her down.

"You need to lie down Tati. I'm not going to hurt you. We had a good time last night and besides I like you," Siren words sounded sincere.

Siren knew in the back of his mind that he didn't know much about Tati, but the vibe was undeniable. In his heart he was ready to settle down but had a hard time finding a woman who understood his lifestyle. The way Tati carried herself said more than any woman he ever came across. He was eager to get to know her.

Tati could hear Siren's voice, but she was having trouble locating his presence. Her head began to spin, and her knees were growing weak. The stress from being home, her son, her mom, and the drama with her friends were finally catching up with her. Siren could see her legs giving out as Tati's body grew limp. He sprinted from the bed just in time to catch Tati in his arms.

"Yo, you good ma?" Siren asked as he sat back on the bed still holding Tati in his arms.

Tati began to cry like a newborn baby as Siren held her.

He could feel some things were off with her but he couldn't put his finger on it. He was unsure if it was a reaction from the drugs or if shawty was just out of it.

"I'm such a fuck up!" Tati screamed.

"No you're not ma. You got to chill," Siren tried to reassure her. He tried his best to calm her down.

"I am!" Tati said.

She didn't realize what she was doing before it was too late. She was so caught up in her emotions which allowed her to speak unspeakable things. "I just came home from jail, like yesterday," Tati said in between cries. "That's why you never seen me around her before.

Siren didn't say a word he just listened. He rocked her slowly and let her get all of her feelings out.

"My best friend was supposed to be looking after my son and my mom's while I was gone, and she didn't. My lights were cut off, and I may lose my house if I don't come up with twenty-five thousand dollars in two days," Tati continued. "And then my other best friend is having a baby with my baby father. They been fucking around while I'll been locked up.

"Damn that's fucked," Siren said, wiping her tears.

Him himself had his shares of fuck ups, but he couldn't relate to her pain. He was born a hustler and the life of a known street thug. To him, Tati problems sounded like a bunch of girl drama, something he likes to stay away from.

"Don't let it get you down ma. I can help with the house thing, like I said I like you and I don't mind helping but that shit with your baby daddy is a lost cause babygirl. You gotta let that go," Siren said sincerely.

Tati sat up slowly and looked into his eyes. She didn't move too fast because she still felt high and her balance was off. "You would do that for me?"

"Yeah ma I would," Siren said.

"I can't take your money. You don't even know me. You just met me," Tati confessed.

"I know ma, but it's something about you," Siren said.

He genuinely felt a connection with her. He had a soft spot for kids, and once he learned that she was in jeopardy losing the house where her son laid his head at night.

"Thank you," Tati whispered. "You don't know what that means to me."

"It's cool. I got you," Siren said. "I'll make all your problems go away."

Tati sat silently for a moment still letting tears stroll down her face. "I just feel like I'm in some shit I can't myself out of.

"What you mean?" Siren asked curiously.

"It's just not the same no more. I usually would do anything for my bitches, especially my bitch Jewel. We've been rocking since kindergarten, but it's different now. I don't know who to trust," Tati said

The alarms went off in Siren head once he heard Jewel's name. He heard about her and her ways in the streets. Always getting a bad vibe from Jewel, and now it put him in position to second guess Tati now.

"These bitches got me doing some foul shit with them in a few days. Jewel done talked both me and Lena into robbing a nigga right before a coke deal this Friday. I don't think I can go through with it," Tati said.

Siren pushed back from Tati as he realized what drop she was talking about. That very same lick was his connection that he hooked Bankroll with. Deep down he knew Jewel was scandalous, but this right here just proves he was always right.

"Yo y'all moving reckless ma. Shit like that will get you killed," Siren said as he stood up to pace his room.

"What's wrong?" Tati asked.

"What's wrong?" Siren asked, confused. "You just sat here and told me you and your bitches are planning to rob my fam."

Tati looked over to Siren in disbelief. She couldn't believe what she just told him. She was pissed off with her friends, but it wasn't like her to be a snitch.

"I didn't know Siren. I'm sorry. I'm such a fuck up," Tati buried her head in her palms.

Siren continued to pace back and forth. He searched the room looking for his phone, he needed to speak to Bankroll Asap to see what he had told his girl. He didn't care that it was almost five in the morning.

"I need to call this nigga." Sire said, picking his phone.

"Call who?" Tati's eyes grew big as she stood up from the bed.

"My nigga Bank!" Siren shouted.

"No. No. No please don't. Please Siren no," Tati pleaded.

"What do you mean no?" You think I'm just sit around and just let y'all rob my shit. That connection is my uncle. My people. My fam," Siren shot bank.

He dialed Bankroll's number and immediately got his voicemail. He tried three more times and got the same result. He decided to send Bank a text message telling him to hit him back ASAP hoping it would be sooner or later.

"Look I know this some fuck up shit, but you got to promise me not say anything. I'll tell Jewel to call it off," Tati pleaded.

"The fact that y'all even thought about it bothers me," Siren admitted. "How can I trust you?"

Tai grabbed Siren hands and placed them on her chest. "I don't want to live this life no more. I'm tired of hurting and disappointing others. It was weighing heavy on me."

Siren knew she had a point. She trusted him enough to tell him the truth even if it was a mix up. "Look I'll give you one day to call this shit off. If not, you're going to be burying your girls. You hear me?"

Tati knew he was serious. She could see the fire burning in his eyes. She only met him a few hours ago, but she felt a connection she couldn't deny.

"I'll handle it," Tati said.

Climbing back in bed, there was an awkward silence between the two. Tati's thoughts consumed her mind. There was only limited time she had to figure out a way to explain to Jewel how she gave up the entire scheme. She was only mad at her friends and never expected to betray them in this way. Since earlier today, the friendship was rocky. She didn't know where the friendship stood, but it was definitely over now.

Chapter 11

Knock. Knock.

Jewel woke up the next morning to the sound of knocking on Bankroll's front door. The couple had fallen asleep together on the couch. Bankroll reached for the remote to check his security cameras on the tv.

"Who the fuck coming by my house this early?"

Jewel sat up straight on the couch as she let out a small yawn and adjusted her eyes toward the tv. Her eyes still felt heavy from lack of sleep. Juan was standing on the porch waiting for someone to answer the door.

"This nigga sho' now how to come by early," Bankroll said as he headed to the door.

Jewel pulled out her phone and noticed she had a message from Lena.

Jewel smiled at her messages before closing. She was anxious to call Lena right now to get the details but didn't want to risk Bankroll walking in. She figured he would be making moves soon, since Juan stopped by. Giving her enough time to be able to handle her business with her girls.

Jewel noticed Bank left his phone next to the couch. Like any curious woman she grabbed the open to find any additional evidence she could use to their advantage for the lick. She hit the side button causing the phone to light up and display miss calls and a Text message from Siren.

Jewel ignored the calls, but it was the text message that caught her attention.

Yo B! I told you that bitch Jewel was foul. I need you to hit me back ASAP.

The message caused Jewel's face to frown up. She didn't know exactly what Siren had against her. She had no idea what Siren knew but she didn't want to take my chances. She attempted Bankroll's password several times causing the phone to self-lock.

"Fuck!" She thought to herself

She looked up at the tv and saw the two men still conversing on the porch, She needed to get inside of Bank's phone to delete the message before he could see it. She instantly looked down at the water on the coffee table from last night. Quickly picking up the glass, she poured the water of the phone causing the screen to go completely black.

"Perfect," Jewel said.

She watched as the two men dap each other up and Juan headed back to his car. Jewel put on sad demeanor so she could play her role. She was even able to form some tears. Bank came back inside with his mind in a daze.

"Baby please don't be mad," Jewel hanged her head low.

'What's wrong baby?" Bank asked.

"I was moving too fast, trying to make it to the bathroom and I accidentally spilled my water all over your phone," Jewel handed him the damaged phone.

Bank examined the phone without saying a word. He looked it over and then tossed the phone to the couch. "It's cool bae, I can replace that."

Jewel smiled that didn't cause a scene. She was glad her plan worked and figured it would buy her some time to handle Siren correctly.

"I need to handle some business really quick. Here's some money. Go handle some business and pick up a new phone" Bank said as he handed her all hundreds and kissed her on the forehead.

Before Jewel could even say thank you, Bankroll disappeared out the front door.

****

****

Later that afternoon Jewel met up with Lena at a local nail salon to pamper herself. It was much needed. The stress from planning the robbery completely stressed her. The risk of losing her life took a toll on her, but her struggles did the same.

"Bitch I needed this," Lena said as she sat back in the massage with her eye closed.

The nail tech massage each toe one by one as her other foot soaked in the warm water, She was sipping on a glass of champagne and eating fruit from a display tray.

'Girl who you telling," Jewel responded. "I tried to call Tati ass because she didn't answer. She needed to call me back so we can get this shit together.

"I'm sure she is," Lena said.

Just as the nail technicians were finishing up, Jewel signaled for them to give the girls some privacy. She needed to talk business with her friend and didn't need any extra ears listening in on her conversation.

"So, I see you got the address," Jewel said in a low whisper.

"Yeah I did bitch, and I almost lost my damn life," Lena said in all seriousness.

Jewel let out a laugh. "And what the hell happened? How did you manage to pull that off?"

"Well of course I put it on him you know that. When we were finished he went into the bathroom and snuck his phone," Lena said.

"He just left his phone out?"

"Yeah girl with no passcode or nothing, but he walked in on me girl. Caught me red handed going through his shit," Lena confessed.

"Wow and what did he do?" Jewel asked.

"He got mad and cursed me out. And that's about it and then he left," Lena said telling only half of the truth.

"Damn, you lucky he ain't do shit else to your ass," Jewel said.

"Yeah girl I know. This baby really saved my ass." The girls both let out a laugh.

The techs return to finishing their jobs. Both ladies sat in relaxation as polish hit their toes. Once they were finished, Jewel pulled out a stack of bills and paid for both services for the ladies. She tipped each tech and thanks them for the great job they did.

"Girl thank you for paying for me. You didn't have to," Lena said.

"I know but you're my girl, I always got you," Jewel said as she placed her arm around her best friend. "Wait before you go."

Lena followed her friend to her car. Jewel pressed the button to cause the trunk to pop. Inside was a decent size brown box hidden under a few clothes in Jewel's trunk. She opened the box revealing semi-automatic pistols and handguns along with ak47s.

"Bitch where did you get these?" Lena asked.

"I purchased them. "Jewel took the money that Bankroll had given her earlier to purchase new weapons. "They're dirty too. So if anything pops off they can't trace them back to us."

Lena picked one up as she admired the pistol. It wasn't something she was used to, but she knew that it was needed. They were going up against two of the biggest drug dealers in the city, so they needed to be strapped.

"Damn bitch. You went all out," Lena said.

"I had too," Jewel took the pistol from Lena's hand, placed it back in the box and closed the trunk. "Look, I'm about to head out. Try to get in touch with Tati and meet me later at my spot.

"Okay." The two girls hugged, and Jewel hoped in her car sped off.

Chapter 12

Tati woke up the next morning feeling ashamed at her actions. Her head was spinning from the long night and her body still felt weak. Tossing and turning throughout the night caused her not to get much sleep and she was feeling anxious. Concern filled her body as she wondered what Siren's next move was and how she would be the cause of her two longest friends' demise. Siren spent the rest of the night pacing the room anticipating his next move as he continuously called Bankroll throughout the night with no answer.

Tati noticed Chico and Loc were no longer laying at the foot of the bed, and the bedroom was slightly cracked. She was hoping Siren was just taking them for a walk to clear his mind. Tati sat on the edge of the bed as she looked around and noticed

Siren car keys were missing from the night stand where he had placed them the night before. She remembered that he put his pistol in the drawer, and she quickly scrambled to open the night stand. There was no sight of the 9mm handgun. Quickly, Tati gathered her belongings, she slipped back into her dress as fast she could with her phone in her hand.

"Shit!" Tati yelled. "I got to get to Jewel fast!"

The house was quiet, that Tati could hear her own heart pounding through her chest. Her breathing became irregular as her palms began to sweat. Looking down, at her phone she noticed she had several messages from Jewel asking to meet up. Before she responded, Tati made an attempt to dial Siren's number, but realized the two didn't have a chance to exchange numbers.

"Fuck!" Tati said.

"What's wrong love?" Tati turned to see Siren standing in the doorway.

"Where have you been?" Tati asked as her perfectly arched eyebrow raised in confusion. "I was looking all over for you?"

"I had some business to handle," Siren said calmly as he placed his keys on the nightstand.

Siren was dressed in all black from head to toe. He removed an oversized pair of gloves from his hands. He was barefoot wearing only a pair of black socks. It was evident that he was up to no good. Both Chico and loc entered in behind him and laid peacefully at the foot of the bed without making a sound.

"What did you do?" Tati pleaded.

"I told you I had some business to handle. What's up with you ma? You alright?" Siren asked

"No I'm not alright. What did you do?" Tati asked, becoming frantic.

He removed his clothing, leaving only his boxers on before stepping inside an oversized closet. Tati listened as he rummaged through his closet. In her soul she could feel he wasn't being completely honest with and feared for her life. Stepping closer to the closet, she peeked and watched him put on new clothing.

"You gone tell me what's up or just gone keep bull shitting me?" Tati asked. "And don't lie to me."

Siren dressed silently before walking past Tati. "Nothing is up," Siren said coldly.

"Look I know I just met you last night you, but do I need to be afraid or what? Did you do something to my friends?" Tati pleaded with tears formed in her eyes

Siren put on a fresh pair of J's that was still in the box. He laced his shoes up as he shook his head. "Your friends? Them hoes ain't your friend baby girl. And you right we did just meet last night, but I have no reason to lie to you."

"What did you do to them?" Tati attempted to shake him, but Siren just pulled back.

"I didn't do shit...yet," Siren said nonchalantly.

Tati stared at him for a moment. She was taken back by his demeanor and his tone. She had only known him for a few hours, but she was smart enough to know he wasn't fucking around.

"Did you talk to Bankroll?" Tati asked.

"Nigga didn't answer. But I will," Siren answered. "Get your shit together."

"Where are we going?" Tati asked as she slipped on her heels from last night.

Siren didn't answer at first. He stood in front of his mirror as he put on his jewelry. He was completely dressed in a whole new outfit and laced with his best jewelry.

"I'm taking you to breakfast ma," Siren said facing her. "Then I'm going to take you shopping. You look like the club."

Tati forced a smile on her face. Deep down inside she was excited for the much-needed shopping trip, but she couldn't help but feel that she sold her friends out for some new clothes and new dick.

"Why are you doing this?" Tati asked.

"I told you last night I liked you. Besides, as long as you're loyal to me, you'll be taken care of ," Siren kissed her cheek sending chills up her spine. "I took care of your little house payments as well. You and yours are good ma."

Tati was grateful for his generosity. She returned the kiss, but this time on Siren's lip. He gripped her ass with one hand as he used the other hand to pull her close.

"Thank you," Tati whispered.

"Thank me later. Let's ride."

****

****

They drove to Waffle House and ate breakfast together and Tati ordered the All-Star Breakfast to soak some of the liquor from the night before. Siren watched as Tati ate as if she hadn't eaten in days.

"Slow down baby girl. If you want, we can order more," Siren said.

Tati placed the fork down and wiped her mouth. She was slightly embarrassed. "I'm sorry. I'm just really hungry. I haven't had good food like this in a while."

"I understand," Siren said. He took a sip of his coffee.

"Look, so I've been thinking all morning about what you told me, and I got to be honest. It's really fucking with me," Siren placed both of his hands on the table and slightly leaned in.

Tati sat with a trouble look on her face. She looked over both of her shoulders before she responded. "I know it is Siren."

"I really want to handle you and your girls. I shouldn't even be fucking with a bitch like you, but I can tell this type of shit its really eating at you," Siren said.

He was right. The more time Tati spent away she realized this life wasn't for her. Even though jackin' niggas was the reason that landed her behind bars, she knew that was her plan that night. She realized how much she put her family in danger with her lifestyle, especially her son.

"It is. And it doesn't make it any better now that these bitches acting funny with me," Tati admitted.

"With that being said, you need to start looking out for yourself ma!" Siren said still leaning toward her, making sure no one could hear him but Tati. "Those tears last night let me know you want to change.

"What do you mean?" Tati asked.

"Tell me the plan and I'll make sure you're safe. I can't have my boy going out like that," Siren pleaded.

Tati pushed her food from in front of her. She thought about her words before she spoke them. "Siren I have to keep it real with you. I would love to help you, but I can't."

Siren's eyebrows raised as he eyed her up and down. "Don't be dumb ma."

Tati felt a little offended by his words, but she didn't let it get to her. She kept her composure. "I can't tell you the plan because I don't know it. We have not discussed it."

Siren paused before letting a small laughter. "You mean to tell me you broads planning to rob some niggas and don't even have a plan."

Tati let out laugh as well. "Well yeah. I'm sure Jewel has something up a sleeve I just don't know yet."

Siren shook his head. "Well whatever she has planned just stick with up until the very last minute. I'm going to protect and make sure they get what they have coming to them."

Tati could feel her stomach turn at the sound of Siren's words. She was pretty sure she knew what Siren meant by his words, but the mother in her couldn't stomach the thought of death for Lena's unborn.

"Get them bitches to go through with the plan, and I'll handle the rest," Siren said.

He pulled out a stack of money and placed it on the table. He stood next Tati and waited for her to get up out of her seat. He grabbed her hand and led her outside to the car. Opening her door, Tati slid inside and sat quietly.

"Remember ma, If you stay loyal to me I will protect you. Ain't no such things as best friends in this game."

Chapter 13

Tre stood on the corner outside of the corner pantry. He figured he would post for a few hours to let his customers know he was up and running and then head back to post up at the trap. Tre had come from a family of hustlers and his father taught him how to be up bright and early trappin' in the streets. Just like his father, he often looked for love in all of the wrong places, so he strictly focused on his money and his respect from the streets to fulfill him

When he first met Tati at sixteen he had no urge to settle down. He was dating many different girls around the city, but Tati held him down. She blessed him with a son that would carry his family name of hustlers around the way. Micah was a spitting image of him from the top of his to the bottom of his feet. He often thought about the baby he created with Lena. He enjoyed his time with Lena, but he knew deep down inside she wasn't the woman for him.

Tre never intended to get Lena pregnant. To him the loyal vibe was never there for him. She was dishonest and often disloyal to her kind. He couldn't trust Lena the way he trusted Tati. The love was different. Even though he showed his gratefulness for the information she provided on her homegirl Jewel and her plan, his gut feeling made him think differently about Lena's motives. He knew Lena was in on the plan, but he just couldn't prove it. Lena and Jewel were thick as thieves, so if Jewel was planning to hit a nigga up, Tre knew Lena was down to ride and for that Lena couldn't be trusted.

Tre stood there consumed in his thoughts as a black SUV slowly pulled into the corner store parking lot. Not recognizing the vehicle, Tre clutched his 9mm tightly on his waist. The passenger side window slightly rolled down just enough to see the driver's eyes.

"Get in!" The driver yelled toward Tre.

"Get in?! Motherfucker I don't know you. If it's a problem you get out!" Tre yelled back getting into his stance.

Tre stood tall ready to blast anybody that got out of line right in broad daylight. Living this life he didn't take any chances. Just as Tre waited for the other party to make a move the back window rolled down.

He didn't recognize the face, but he knew the voice. "Get inna di cyar!" Sunny shouted toward Tre heavy in his Jamaican accent.

"Fuck!" Tre mumbled under his breath as he walked toward the car. Tre got in the car on the passenger side, with Sonny sitting directly behind him. As soon as he closed the door the car sped off, not giving Tre any time to object.

"What's good Sonny?" Tre asked nervously.

He often heard stories on how ruthless the Jamaican cartel was and never wanted to be on their bad side. It was in their blood to be gangsters. In the early seventies, his family moved across the country and ran the most lucrative drug cartel in the streets of Miami.

Sonny took a puff of the cigar in his hand. He inhales deeply, slowly exhaling the smoke from his nostrils. The gas was so strong as it filled the air in the car, it caused the other passengers to choke from it. "Yuh tell mi mon."

"Man ain't shit. I'm just out here gettin it like always man." Tre said, rubbing his palms against his leg.

"Yuh seem nervous mon." Sonny wore a pair of dark Gucci shades hiding his eyes, but his body gesture said a lot.

"Nah I'm cool. Just a little surprise to this visit?"

"Tell mi how a everyting wid fi mi ittle biznizz transaction? Sonny asked with the cigar still lit in his hands.

"Everything is everything. I got everything handled and ready to go. Bank still looking to buy." Tre said.

"A dat right?" Sonny took a puff and inhaled the smoke. "Suh enuh nutten bout sum bitches planning tuh rob mi ah fi mi coke an fi mi money?"

Tre raised his eyebrow in confusion as he listened to Sonny's question. He seemed puzzled at the question. He had no knowledge of anyone planning to rob him. "Man Sonny I don't know what you talking about. I haven't heard shit! Especially about some bitches."

Sonny took a long pause, never looking in Tre's direction. "A yuh fucking wid mi bwoy?"

"Nah. Never." Tre said, attempting to plead his case. He was never afraid to stand his ground, but he knew better than anyone not to play with Sonny.

"Fi mi criss nephew let mi kno bout ah plan dat ah few dees raggedy bitches roun yah hab plan tuh rob mi ah fi mi product. An mi kno fi mi nephew wouldn't lie tuh mi," Sonny said, sitting up straight, finally facing Tre.

"Man I'm lost. I have no idea what you're talking about. I haven't heard anything." Tre pleaded.

"Fi mi nephew did tell mi bout ah ooman named Jewel an har fren dem. A ih true?" Sonny asked.

Tre eyes grew big at the sound of Jewel's name. His thoughts begin to crowd him as he thought about the questioning from Lena the other day. He didn't think twice about their conversation until now. "Bitch"

"What?!" Sonny asked.

"Nothing man. Look I ain't heard nothing about no females planning to jack me for your shit. I swear man." Tre said, growing irritated. He was ready to end this conversation and go pay Lena and her home girls a visit.

"Tap di car!." Sonny shouted, causing the car to come to immediate halt.

Tre's body slung back and forth causing his head to hit the window. "Ahh fuck man!"

Sonny gripped Tre by his neck, causing his airway to stop as he puts his cigar out on Tre's face. "Nuh fuck wid mi bwoy!"

Tre sat there screaming in agony from the irritation of pain from the pain. "Fuck Sonny. I told you I didn't know shit man."

"I nuh believe yuh. Yuh betta handle dis. Eff any ting is fucked up, mi will kill yuh miself. Now git out of mi car!" Sonny released Tre's neck as he kicked out of the SUV.

The car sped off, as Tre sat on the ground trying to catch his breath. "I'm going to kill that bitch…"

Chapter 14

After breakfast together, Siren drop Tati off to her crib. He told her to get something together and to meet him back at his place later. He was able to convince her to go along with the plan to set her girls up in exchange for a new life with her son.

He could tell that Tati was a little skeptical at first for she didn't seem like the type to turn against her girls, but Siren knew she wanted a better life. He didn't care about her nasty drug habit. He knew when the time was right, he hoped to wing her off that shit and get her life in order for her son.

Siren was a trained killer. He was taught to be a goon, someone who taught to murk anybody if there was an issue, including women. He spent half of his morning trying to get in contact with Bank to give him a heads up about his bitch but seem to have no luck. He knew this was some shit, with a little help from Tati, he would have to handle on his own.

He headed back to his crib to get his mind together and to wait for Tati's call. He knew he needed to be on a hit for he had no idea how Jewel and Lena was coming. With an inside connect he was confident this would end his favor.

Like a true soldier he was able to send a message to his uncle Sonny and assured him, he would be the one handling business for him. He was determined to set Dixianna on fire behind his fam. He was uncertain of the part Tre played in all of this, but he knew his nigga Bank was blinded by a scandalous bitch.

Siren pulled up to his crib. He hopped out the car and headed to the door. As he approached the door, he could feel something was off. With his right hand on piece, Siren tip-toed toward the back of the house. He reached for his cellphone to check the security footage. Nothing.

Placing the phone back into his pocket, Siren walked to the back yard and noticed a large box sitting in the middle of the yard. The box was simply labeled with a note attached to the outside, "Blood ain't that thick." across the front. He quickly drew his weapon and pointed it to each angle as he watched his surroundings.

He fired a few rounds at the box to see if it would blow up. Once he realized it wasn't a bomb he removed the picket knife from his pocket and sliced the tape on the box. The top flew open, revealing both Chico and Los dead inside.

"Ahh shit! Fuck!" Siren said. "Who the fuck would do this?"

Siren shut the top of the box and headed inside through the back with his gun still drawn. He was baffled that he allowed someone to get this close to him to do this. He crept through the house quietly hoping to catch whoever did this.

He checked each inch of the house with no sign of anyone. There was nothing out of place. Siren placed his gun on the counter as he gathered his thoughts. It was evident to him that whoever was responsible for this was trying to deliver a message, and the message was received.

Chapter 15

Tati sat back on her bed as she thought about Siren's proposition. She was tired of this lifestyle and wanted better for herself and son. In the few short hours she spent with Siren, deep down she knew he would eb a man that could take care of her. To provide and protect her.

Siren was able to pay her light bill up for a year as well as her house payment. The gesture alone showed her she could depend on him. With a smile on her face she began to pack a few clothes and shoes in a bag. She planned to return back to Siren's house to be with him.

"Going somewhere again?" Tati's mom entered her room holding baby Micah in her arms.

"Jesus mom, you scared me," Tati said as she placed her hand on her heart.

"You've yet to answer the question girl."

"I'm leaving for a few days, ma. I'll be back," Tati answered, rushing to zip her bag hoping to avoid the conversation that was coming.

"You just got home, and you have barely spent any time with this baby. He barrel knows you Tati!" Her mother shouted.

"My son knows me. Besides I'm handling business so I can give him a better life."

"Ain't that much business need handling in the world Tati. You need to be seeing about this baby." Her mother said.

"Ma, I am, and I will," Tati said, changing her tone hoping to lighten the mood. "Just give me some time."

Tati's mother rolled her eyes as she left the room. Tati flopped on the bed and let out a deep sigh. She pulled out her phone to check her messages. She sent a text to Siren's phone. She was eager to get back to him even though she just left him. She felt safe with him.

Ring. Ring.

Tati's phone began to ring. It was Jewel. She hoped up from the bed to close her down before answering the call.

"Hello."

"Bitch why are you whispering?" Jewel asked in annoyed tone,

"I ain't trying to talk loud, Micah sleeping," Tati lied.

"Oh. Well where have you been bitch. Lena and I both have been trying to get up with you," Jewel asked.

"I've been around Jewel. I had some business to handle," Tati lied again.

"Well whatever bitch," Jewel said. Quickly changing the subject. "We're still on for later tonight right? We can count on you.

Tati could feel her stomach caving in as she grew sick. Her palms began to sweat, and her heart raced to Jewel's question. Her loyalty has always been to her two best friends, but lately it didn't seem the bond was so tight anymore.

"I don't know Jewel. We may need a little more too.."

"Bitch I know you're not flaking on me?" Jewel interrupted her. "You know the deal Tati. Besides we need you.

"You and Lena seem to have everything under control. What do you need me for?" Tati asked.

"Bitch, it was your idea to start robbing niggas in the first place," Jewel said, as her tone shifted. "Stop acting like a punk ass bitch and get your mind together.

Tati was heated at Jewel for her words. Deep down she was tired of robbing and scheming to get ahead. She was ready to live a legit life, but that didn't make her no punk ass bitch.

"Fuck you Jew. I ain't no punk ass bitch!" Tati screamed into the phone. "I am just simply telling that this ain't it. We need a better plan."

"We have a plan. It's simple. We pull up to the spot, scope it out, wait for the drop, rush them niggas, grab the money and drugs and be out," Jewel said with confidence.

"And what makes you think Bankroll won't shoot dead once he finds out it's you?" Tati asked.

"He ain't gone find out shit. And if he does, I'll be long gone before he realizes it was even me," Jewel said.

In Jewel's mind, the plan was perfect. There was no doubt in her mind that she couldn't pull this off. In the past, they've hit many victims with more to lose, and Tati was always on go. This new found attitude was confusing to Jewel.

"Lena gave me the rundown. This money we back to jack is chump change to these niggas. They're not going to miss the money Tati," Jewel said.

"I hear you. I just think we should think about it more," Tati continued.

Jewel took a long pause before speaking. "There's nothing to think about. Get your shit together and meet me at my house in the next few hours. You owe me. So don't fucking play with me."

Jewel ended the call. Tati sat on the bed and buried her face into her hand. Her phone begin to ring again. She could feel her stomach growing sick at the thought of Jewel calling back. She glanced at the phone and noticed it was Siren calling.

"Hello."

"I need you ma. You ready?" Siren asked, not even greeting her.

"Almost. I'll be back over in an hour," Tati said.

"I need you now," Siren pleaded.

Tati could hear the discomfort in his tone. "What's wrong?"

"So much ma. I just need you here Asap," Siren pleaded once more.

Tati paused as she thought about her next move. "I'm on the way."

Chapter 16

Siren sat in his study with his henchmen standing around, filling each corner of the room. He spent the next few hours going over the security footage trying to figure who the intruders were. He rubbed his goatee as he rewind and fast forward through the footage. He couldn't seem to identify the masked figure, who invaded his privacy.

Growing frustrated, Siren poured himself a glass of scotch as he waited for Tati's arrival. "Yo, any of you niggas spoke with Bank today?" Siren asked.

Each goon shook their head, indicating that no one had spoken to him. It was usual for the duo to check in with each other. Siren had spent most of his day reaching out to his friend, only to be unsuccessful.

"It's not like this nigga to hit me back," Siren spoke out loud, but to himself.

He picked up his office phone to dial Bankroll's number. The call was sent straight to voicemail. Siren slammed the phone down on his desk. He massaged his temples to release his chest. He pulled out a cigar from his top drawer to smoke. The smoke invaded his lungs as he inhaled and exhaled.

"We got to catch the mother fuckers that did this ," Siren said, as he pounded his desk with a close fist.

Siren was slightly hurt behind his pet dogs, but he wasn't planning on losing any sleep. He was more concerned with his respect and how he allowed someone to even get that close to him. Siren slouched back into his office chair as he massaged his goatee. The loud noise from the ringing of the phone in his ear caused him to snap out of his daze.

"Yo!" Siren spoke into the phone

"What's good fam?" Tre asked in a muffled tone. "We're still good for tonight?"

"Yeah, we're straight," Siren answered.

"Cool. Cool." Tre responded. "Aye have heard anything from that nigga Bank? I can't seem to get in touch with him."

Siren sat up in his chair as he seemed to focus on Tre's words. Tati made her way in to Siren's office wearing a skin tight nude dress that hugged her entire frame. Her hair was pulled into a neat ponytail that showed the beautiful features of her bare face. Siren smiled as a greeting to her.

"To my understanding every still copasetic. I haven't been able to get in touch with the fool all day," Siren confessed.

"Man that's crazy." Tre said. "I need to give him a heads up about things. I need everything to run smoothly tonight. Ya feel me?"

"I feel you fam. I need the same man," Siren said.

Tati swayed her hips toward Siren's desk. His henchman dismiss themselves as they watch Tati make herself comfortable on top of his desk, directly in front of him. She spread her legs, placing each leg on each of his shoulders, locking them together. Sirens manhood instantly raised as he eyed her pretty pearl in between her legs.

"One on the street its some bitches planning to rob us tonight, and I need to make sure Bank ain't in on this. I'm in no mood to fuck up my connections or my money behind any bitch." Tre said in a serious tone.

Siren slightly pushed Tati away as he listened. His eyebrows raised in a slight concern. He was aware of the same knowledge from Tati the night before. "I hear you fa. And trust me I have all of that under control," Siren said.

"Oh yeah?" Tre asked.

"Yeah," Siren stated. "Trust me they're not going to get away with this. I got something from them bitches.

Tati's body sifted up as she listened to Siren's conversation. She had no idea who he was talking to, but she knew he was talking about them. She hopped off the desk and pulled her dress down and made her way to the other side of the desk. She sat patiently and quietly in the chair as Siren continued.

"Just make you meet in the spot tonight," Siren said, ending the conversation.

Even though he felt he could trust Tati, he was no fool. He trusted she chose the right side, but he didn't want to risk her switching sides at the last minute. He couldn't let her know too much.

"Aight, bet." Tre said. "I got some things to handle but I'll be there."

"Bet," Siren hung the phone up and paused for a minute.

Finally he directed his attention to Tati. She was checking her face in a small compact mirror to bypass the time. She noticed him staring at her from the corner of her eye.

"Everything good?" She asked, knowing the answer.

"Everything will be," Siren said, as he stood up to head toward her

The sight of her made his man solid. She was sexy in her own way, even though she had some issues. He was willing to fix anything that she would allow him to. He stood directly in front of her.

"I'm glad to hear that," Tati smiled. "You want me to make you feel better?"

"And just how are you going to do that?" Siren asked, as he leaned back on the desk with his arms folded.

Tati sat up straight as she pressed her weight on the chair to seductively move to her knees. Making eye contact with her lover, she unbuckled then unzipped his pants revealing his manhood. Standing directly at attention, she stroked his ego with her right-hand causing Siren to relax.

With saliva dripping from her perk lips, she took Siren inside of her mouth. Her tongue simultaneously tickled his balls as Siren gripped the back of her head. He motioned her head back and forth, up and down in a grove.

"You the truth ma," Siren said.

Tati's moan filled the air as she focused on the task at hand. She gripped his legs, so she could keep up with Siren's groove. She licked and slurped, throwing her head back and forth aiming to please her new man.

"That's right baby. Make daddy relax," Siren said in between his moans.

Tati continued her performance. Siren gripped her ponytail tightly that she knew his ending was near.

Before Tati could pull away, Siren released himself into her mouth. Like a pro she slurp and swallow every drop. She stood and wipe her mouth with the back of her hand. She smirked as Siren regained his self.

"Damn I needed that," Siren smiled back.

Tati leaned in to whisper in his ear. "I'm going to go and freshen up for you daddy."

Tati made her way outside of the office and headed to the master bedroom where she spent the night before. She made herself at home as she plopped on the bed. She thought about her life, her friends and most of all Siren. She was feeling him. There was no way she could go through with the plan tonight. There was no way she could betray her new found man.

Chapter 17

Lena entered her house with grocery bags filled in one hand. She was extremely exhausted and eager to lay down. As she walked in she noticed the flickering lights from the candles that were burning inside her home. The smell of incense filled each room causing her to instantly be relaxed.

She dropped her purse and groceries right at her feet as she stood stunned at the nice gesture in front of her. Red and White rose petals placed in a trail leading her into the kitchen area where she saw a glass of wine waiting for her. Besides Jewel, Tre was the other only person who had the keys to her place. Soft sounds of Changing Faces's *Stroke You Up* played in the background.

Do you mind if I stroke you up (I don't mind), Do you mind if I stroke you down (I don't mind), All

Roses filled her countertop completely covering her tiles. Lena came overjoyed at the scenes she leaned in to smell her flowers. Tre was putting a true effort forward to woo her. Giving her the hope that he was ready to be fully committed to her.

"Ouu baby, you shouldn't have," Lena said to herself.

Making her way toward her stairs, she pulled her shirt over her head and began unbuttoning her jeans as she walked slowly and seductively toward her room. The music grew louder.

"This is my song baby," Lena called out as she sang along to the music. *"Do you mind if I stroke you down (I don't mind).*

Entering the bed room, the entire room lit solely from the candles. Tears formed her eyes as she slid her jeans to the floor. Her perky breast sat at attention. She looked around for Tre but she didn't see him.

She walked to the master bathroom and peeked inside. There was no Tre in sight, but she did take notice to the bath that was ran for her.

"He's really scoring major points," Lena said aloud as she reached for her robe from behind the bathroom door.

"Lena."

Lena jumped at the sound of the voice; she was startled. "Jesus Tre. You scared me," Lena said.

"My bad baby girl," Tre said, as he took a step closer. He leaned forward and looked into her eyes before kissing her lips."

"It's okay baby," Lena said, trying to catch her breath. "All of this is so nice."

Tre rubbed the side of Lena's face. "Have I told you how beautiful you are?"

Lena smiled at his words. She was so happy at that moment. She always wanted to know Tre's true feelings for her, and he was finally showing her. She kissed his again, this time shoving his tongue inside of his mouth. Their tongues danced together as chills crept her spine sending her lady parts into overdrive

Tre untied her robe allowing it to drop to her feet, causing her to be fully naked again. He walked over to her vanity and sat her down. She faced toward the mirror and closed her eyes, placing her hands on the mirror. Tre kissed her neck softly and whispered in her ear.

"Remember what you told me the other day about your homegirl? I just wanted to reward you for that." Tre confessed.

"That was nothing baby, you know I always have your back," Lena said back.

She was still feeling guilty on the inside for turning on her girl, but she was enjoying this new Tre. she knew she would have to face Jewel for her betrayal soon. A part of her felt bad for the lies she told to Tre, but she was willing to sacrifice her friendship for Tre's love.

"I will always reward loyalty." Tre said massaging her shoulders. "We both know your loyal baby girl, but you're loyal to the wrong one babygirl."

Lena opened her eyes and stared directly into Tre's through the mirror. " What.. What are you talking about?" Lena turned toward him.

Tre looked down and shocked his head. He smacked Lena across the face with the back of his hand so hard, causing her to grip the side of her face.

He pulled a small rag from his pocket. Lena's eyes grew wide as she eyed his every move. Her heart began to race and beat faster than before. Before she could move to run, Tre gripped her neck putting her in a headlock forcing the rag over her mouth.

Lena kicked as she tried to move from his hold. Her brain was telling her to scream but each second she grew weak. The rat poison on the rag caused her to grow faint as her body became numb in his arms. Still holding her by the neck, Tre dragged Lena inside the bath room to the tub. Lena couldn't fight back she was to weak.

Forcefully, Tre shoved Lena's ahead below the water, causing her to submerge the water. Roughly grabbing her hair, he Lifted her head up to see that she wasn't breathing. Shoving her head in one last time, he held her down, this time longer. "I know you were in on it bitch. And here's a little free game, a baby don't keep no nigga."

Chapter 18

Bankroll pulled up to Juan's trap house and got out cautiously. He knew after the drop tonight, him and Jewel would be going ghost for a while. He was ready to focus on the baby and give Jewel a settled a lifestyle. He was still down a phone but had no worries of replacing it. He made a mental note to replace once they got to where they were going.

Anxiety filled his gut as he approached the door. An uneasy feeling crowded him, but he quickly shook the feeling. When the two of them got together it was always love. They instantly click like brothers, after Juelz death Bank took Juan under his wing looking out for him any way he could.

Bank stepped inside the crack house as he eyed each person in the room. He gripped his pistol on his hip and as he searched for Juan. Bank knew that Juan oversaw the family business, dealing crack to the locals, but he never imagined being this hands on. He spotted the regulars getting high in the corners and some begging for their next hit.

Bank spotted Juan in the kitchen cooking his product while another hustler bagged the product. "What's good bruh."

"Oh shit you made it?" Juan said as he approach Bank to greet him

"Yeah I just had to make a stop and then I was on the way," Bank said.

"True. True. My bad for pulling you away from your lady friend, but I didn't want to talk business there," Juan admitted.

"I got you fam. I understand. It's something women don't need to be a part of ," Bank said.

"Facts." Both men laugh as they dapped each other up.

"What you got goin in here, fam?" Bank asked as he eyed the scene again. "It's never good to mix business with pleasure.

Bank stared directly at Juan hoping he was catching his drift. Juan caught on, but he wanted to explained his position. He allowed his customers to get high in his trap house that way, once that first high came down the wouldn't have to travel far for that second helping. Even though it was risky, Juan wasn't a fool. He had men lined up and armed ready to gunned anything or anybody that disrespected him in his place of business.

"It's cool fam. I got it under control," Juan let out a laugh.

"I'm just trying to look out for you fam," Bank said.

"I appreciate that man."

Juan poured himself a glass of Hennessey as well as one for Bank roll. Then two men clicked glasses and down the drink within seconds. They sat at the table next to the guy who was bagging Juan's product. Juana shot the young hustler a look letting himself know to dismiss himself from the room.

Once they were alone Juan started talking. So what's going on with you man?"

"I'm straight man. What about you? How are you holding up?" Bank asked.

"I'm good man. Living and making money," Juan said, pouring another glass.

"Bet. I'm just asking, being that Tati got out the other day," Bank said, fishing to see where Juan's head was at.

"Yeah, I ain't stuntin' that hoe. She's a lost girl," Juan said.

Juan never expressed his feelings about Tat's involvement for his brother's death. He was fully aware that Tati' was there that night but was unclear exactly what role she played.

Bank laughed. "Yeah she lost alright."

Juan downed his next glass. He noticed one of the feens approaching him. His eyes were wide open, and he seemed to shake uncontrollably. Knowing he needed a hit, Juan faced waiting for the frail man to speak his peace.

"Hey man I just need a loan until next week. I can pay you next week?" The man asked in a begging tone. He was highly irritated and was hoping to catch a break.

"Man what the fuck did I tell you? I don't do loans. You either pay now or get the fuck out," Juan said, slightly raising his voice.

"Man please. Just do an old man a favor." The man continued to beg.

Juan wasn't amused. "Nigga, what did I say?" Juan placed his pistol from the table to his lap as he caress the trigger.

The old man took the hint and inch away back toward his spot next to his wife. He'd been coming to Juan spot ever since his dad ran his joint back in the eighties. He was used to getting "loans" just to feel high, but that was one thing Juan didn't allow once he took over.

"Damn man, you tough," Bank said.

"Got to be. Motherfuckers love to fuck you over," Juan said.

Bank let out a laugh. "So what you called me here for man? You came by the house in the morning saying we need to talk?"

Juan looked around to make sure there were no extra ears paying attention to his next move. He placed his pistol back on the table as he faced Bank in his eyes.

"Your man Siren… how do you feel about him?" Juan asked in a serious tone.

"What do you mean? That's my right hand," Bank confessed.

"Yeah I get all that but how well do you know him?" Juan asked.

Bank eyebrows roses in confusion as he looks over to Juan. He has never questioned Siren let alone never questioned Siren's loyalty.

"You know man since about a year ago, after Juelz died," Bank added.

"Exactly. This clown shows up claiming to be blood after my brother passed but I never heard of him," Juan said. "And now he is supposed to be in on the deal you made with my uncle. I don't trust him."

"Yeah he's an equal partner. The coke we planned on purchasing we just splitting down the middle," Bank said.

"You sure about that?" Juan asked, placing his hands on the table.

"Yeah I'm sure," Bank said. "Look fam I don't really like to be questioned. Just tell me what the fuck is going on here."

Juan stood up and paced the trap house. He managed to pour another drink before he spoke. "Siren is planning to cut you completely out of the deal tonight. It's his plan to take both yours and his half of the coke branch out on his on."

Bank bodied filled with rage as he listened. He couldn't believe his ears. Siren has always moved behind him and had his back. Never giving Bank any reason to think he was a flaw.

"What are you talking about J?" Bank asked.

"I need you to hear me. Them fifty G's you about to give Tre tonight for Sonny's coke is only worth twenty-five. Siren and Tre are planning to keep twenty-five-thousand and your coke and expand their business together as partners. And cut you out.

The plan was set for Bank to purchase some of Miami's purest cocaine from Sonny. Bank was leaving the product behind with Siren so he could make a couple of moves to connect with new connections, an idea he got from Siren. It was clear that Siren had different plans.

"How do you know all of this fam?" Bank asked, as his blood began to boil.

"For one I don't have to lie to you," Juan said. "Two, I be watching motherfuckers closely. I know it was something off."

Juan pulled a vanilla folder from the kitchen drawer that contained information inside. It revealed Siren's true identity and family history showing no relation to Sonny whatsoever. Bank slammed his fist on the table as he read the news.

"That fucker tried to fuck me," Bank said as he grip his pistol.

He cock the gun back after he removed the safety. He was ready for war. His target was lurking right under his nose. He was truly torn by the betrayal but his right-hand man, and once he felt betrayed he saw nothing but death.

Chapter 19

Lena laid on her bathroom floor in pain. The knots in her stomach seemed to tighten as each second went by. Her breathing was shallow and fast causing her to over work her body. She had passed out for a few, playing dead hoping that Tre would give up.

Once she knew he was gone, she opened her eyes only to realize she was too weak to move. She cradled her stomach as she thought about her baby.

"Hold on pumpkin. Mama got you." She said in a faint whisper.

She tried to scoot her body to the toilet, to help herself up. Remembering her phone being down stairs, she tried to remain calm. Lena could feel a warm substance between her legs submerge from her outfit. Rubbing her hands down below, her heart fainted when she noticed the blood creeping down her leg.

"Oh my God. NO! NO! NO!" She cried out. "I can't lose my baby."

She managed to crawl toward her bed room only to feel vomit sitting on her chest. She relieved herself all over her white fur carpet. Her blooded handprint stained the carpet as she crawled toward the bed. Her cough increased as she seemed to choke on the air.

"I can't breathe," Lena said, and she fell faint on the floor.

She was trying so hard to push herself to the door, but she was ultimately too weak.

The smell of smoke crept through the bedroom door, causing Lena to choke. She lied on her back, fighting for her life. She let out a cry for help hoping someone could hear her, but it was no use. The smell of gas crept up her nose as the loud sounds of the smoke alarm ringed in her ear.

"My baby! No not my baby," Lena spoke her last words before she closed her eyes.

****

Tati made her way to Jewel's door like she was directed. Her and siren spent hours going over the plan to make sure she understood. She was to act normal during the robbery as if she knew nothing, and he promised she wouldn't be hurt.

Her anxiety reached the pit of her stomach as she rang Jewel's door bell. She was nervous to face Jewel, but she knew what needed to be done. Jewel hadn't been a good friend to her and felt her loyalty was with the man she loved.

"Finally," Jewel said as she rang the doorbell.

Tati stepped in dress in a long trench coat like she was instructed. She was used to seducing a guy to hit a lick, but never approaching her victims head on. This was new for them and Tati didn't feel they were ready.

She felt confident of having Siren on her side, but she was sure about the other men who were present in the game. She didn't have a safe card with them and was afraid they would pop off at the sight of robbers.

"Whatever bitch. I'm here," Tati said in a tone Jewel did not like.

"What's with you?" Jewel asked, catching on to Tai's attitude.

"I'm fine. I'm just ready to get this done. I need to get back to my baby," Tati lied.

Jewel rolled her eyes at Tati's statement. "Yeah, okay."

Tati sat on the edge couch, not to make herself comfortable. "Quick, give me the rundown."

"It's simple. We steak the drop. Wait for the men to approach each other. hop out jack their shit and leave," Jewel said confident,

"That's it? That's your plan?" Tati asked, irritated. "And what if one of these fools pop off on one of us? What the fuck we supposed to do?"

"Pop back," Jewel said, as she walked toward her closet.

Jewel retrieved the weapons and threw Tati's way. Tati's eyes grew big as she looked over the gun. Jewel eyed her weapon as if it was a prize. She cradles it like a newborn baby.

"Where did you get these?" Tati asked

"A friend," Jewel answered.

Tati decided against asking any more questions. She didn't want to give off too much suspicion. Instead she just sat quietly and patiently waited for the move.

"It's almost time. We're just waiting on Lena slow ass," Jewel as she dialed Lena's number.

She specifically told Lena to be there thirty minutes before then she told Tati. She hadn't spoken to Lena since their trip to the salon and it was unlike her not to reach out or to call and say she was late. Jewel reached Lena's voice mail.

"Fuck. Where is she?" Jewel said aloud.

"Probably fucking my baby daddy," Tati said sarcastically, as she pulled a flash from her pocket.

Jewel overheard her comment. "Don't start your shit in here tonight. We got work to do."

Tati rolled her eyes.

"If this bitch doesn't show up, we're going to have to go without her," Jewel said.

Tati's mind felt relieved for that was one less friend's death she would feel responsible for. She took one last sip before putting the flash of whiskey back in her pocket.

"You really need to lay off that shit. It ain't cute," Jewel said never facing Tati.

"It relaxes me," Tati said.

"You're a drunk. No man wants a drunk," Jewel scolded.

The pair waited for Lena's arrival only for her to never show. Jewel moves quickly as she prepared for her night. She made sure all weapons were loaded and that both her and Tati had a mask to cover their faces. They wore gloves for protection.

Jewel drove down Charleston highway toward the interstate in full speed. She lit a blunt to calm her nerves and passed it to Tati. The high begun to settled in as they rode in silence. She dial Lena number one last time, this time leaving her girl a voicemail.

Hey Le. Where the fuck are you? Call me back. Better yet when you hear this, just come to the spot ready.

Jewel hung the phone up. She cut her head lights as she approached the alley of the warehouse. She was able to park her car out of sight only to reveal that they were the first ones there. She noticed that Tati was more quiet than normal as she paid all of her attention to her cellphone.

"I hope your ready bitch. It's just us," Jewel said as look over to Tati.

"I'm always ready. You just keep up."

The Final Chapter

"Make sure you stick the plan and don't fuck shit up," Jewel placed her gun in her lap as she watched Bankroll pull into the location. "Where the fuck is Lena ass."

Jewel had been calling her Lena with no luck. It wasn't like Lena not to return her call or to miss a lick. Deep down she needed her girl here., she trusted Lena more than she trusted Tati and things didn't feel the same.

"Relax. I'm sure She will be here" Tati said as she scrolled on her phone.

She quickly typed a text to Siren, letting him they were here. Her mind was filled with thoughts of Siren. She had only known him for a few days, but she felt close to him. Knowing that he would be a great man to take care of her and her son, and for once she was ready to choose love over her lifestyle. She constantly checked her phone to see if Siren messaged her back Nothing.

Tati sat back in her seat, replaying the plan repeatedly through her head in silence. She was so anxious, and her stomach had minor knots. The plan was simple, but she was more worried of being found sooner than later.

"What can this bitch be doing? She definitely got some explaining to do.?" Jewel said as she locked her phone. "I need her."

"She's probably somewhere throwing up," Tati said laughing making a joke in reference to Lena's pregnancy.

"She better be for her sake," Jewel said. "It's not like her not to text or call back.

Jewel felt it was something off, but she couldn't stomach the thought. They were running out of time. She knew Tre would be here soon. She didn't want any extra guests. She simply wanted to off Bank and Siren smoothly and walk away with the money.

"Fuck it we gotta move now," Jewel removed the safety from her gun.

"Right now?" Tati said nervously looking down at her phone, still no text from Siren.

"Yes. Bank just pulled up. We gotta move now before Tre pulls up. The less the better," Jewel said, taking one last look at Tati.

"But I thought we were jacking the coke too?" Tati asked in confusion.

"So you can smoke it?" We can do it without. Let's move," Jewel said, exiting the car.

Jewel pulled her skully over her face, only revealing her eyes. They were both dressed in long black trench coats and black leather gloves with thigh high boots. Tati took one last sip of alcohol she had left, before doing the same. She tucked her phone in her coat pocket before stepping out of the car.

She noticed Siren's car pulling in directly behind Bank's Car as her phone vibrated. She looked over to Jewel who looked nervous. The two walked toward the car unnoticed. Ducking behind the dumpster, they squatted and waited. Tati could feel her phone buzz in her pocket again but she ignored it.

Siren stepped out the car and walked toward Bank roll's window. The two men begin to converse before Siren returns to his car. The girls watched and waited. It was evident they were waiting for Tre so they could make the drop.

"On the count of three we go," Jewel said.

"Jewel wait…" Tati said, with her heart pounding.

"What?! It's not the time for your bull shit Tati," Jewel snapped.

Siren walked back toward Bankroll's care with two duffel bags in his hand. Jewel eyes filled with money signs.

"One, two, three, go!" Jewel said as she sprinted from behind the dumpster with her pistol in hand. Tati followed. "Don't fucking move."

"What the fuck is this?!" Bank shouted, eyeing the two females with their guns drawn.

Siren pulled his gun from his waist line matching Jewel energy. He looked toward Tati and back to Jewel. Tati pointed her gun toward Bank's car.

"We just want the money, that's it," Jewel said.

Bank paused for a minute as if he recognized the mask figure's voice. "You bitches ain't getting shit," Bank said, hoping out of his car. He was strapped but hadn't pulled his gun yet.

Siren stood at attention with fire in his eyes. He continued to point his gun to Jewel never taking his eyes off of her. She noticed his animosity toward and return the motion.

"Motherfucker if it's smoke then do me something," Jewel said as she eyed Siren.

Siren smirked. "You have no idea."

Bankroll noticed the exchange between the two. "Man you know these broads?"

Siren laughed as he looked at Bank. "You have no idea."

Tati shake uncontrollably as her fingers felt wobbly on her gun. She point her gun toward Bank causing him to draw his gun, but to point it directly toward Siren.

"Give me money G," Bank said ignoring the girls.

"What the fuck are you doing fam?" Siren asked, still pointing his gun toward Jewel.

"Both of you drop your piece or me and my girl are going to blow both of your shit off," Jewel said angry.

Bank continued to ignore her. "You heard me, my guy. Give me my fucking money.

Siren side-eyed his partner as he turned his gun toward him. "You got something on your chest?"

"You tell me?" Bank asked.

Jewel was growing irritated before she knew time was running short. She knew Bank and Siren to be tight and was confused by this exchange that was occurring in front of her.

"What the fuck Jewel?" Tati whispered.

"Helllloooo! Give us the money!" Jewel demanded.

"You ain't getting shit Jewel," Siren said, never taking his eyes off of Bank.

Jewel could feel her stomach sinking to her ass. She was not expecting him to recognize her. Her palms were sweating, and she knew she needed to act fast before Bank did, but it was too late.

"Jewel?" Bank eyes lit with fire. "What the fuck is this.

Bank took a step back as he eyed the situation. He was caught off guard that both his girl and right-hand man had pistol drawn toward him.

"Yeah Nigga, your own bitch is willing to rob you blind," Siren said.

"As well as my right hand," Bank shot back revealing he knew all about Siren's plan.

"Is that right?" Siren challenged.

"That's right." Noticing that Siren wasn't backing down, Bank raised his gun.

"Ughhhhh. I can't take this shit no more!" Tati yelled, turning the attention to her.

At this point, Tati pointed her gun toward Jewel as she moved behind Siren.

"Bitch what are you doing?" Jewel asked confused

"You know what Jewel is. You're flaw," Tati answered.

Siren crew a smirk on his face happy that he had extra bullets on his side. He watched Bank closely ready to buss, if Bank made the wrong move. Growing impatient, Jewel removed her mask revealing her face.

"I'm not playing anymore. Just give me the money," Jewel said. "Besides, I've never had a friend be a friend to me, so the betrayal was expected."

"How could you ma?" Bank asked. "You're carrying my whole seed.

Both Siren and Tati let out a laugh at Bankroll's statement. Revealing her face, Tati answered. "She ain't pregnant bro, she played you."

Bank soul seemed to be crushed when he heard the words. He truly believed that Jewel was carrying his child and we were willing to even spare her.

"Is it true?" Bank asked in a soft tone.

Jewel rolled her eyes just as she was getting ready to speak, gun shots begin to ring out in the distance m, with two bullets hitting her in the back causing her to fall slump face forward.

Bank quickly blasted his gun in the direction of the gun shots, causing Tre to reveal himself. Tre aimed toward Siren hitting him two times in the chest and then toward Bank missing his shot.

Bank fired back as he dragged Jewel's Body behind his vehicle. Tati duck as she struggled to get out of the way. She frantically searches for Siren's keys in his pocket. Bank continued to duck back and forth behind his car, firing shot after shot. Billets bounce on and off of Bankroll's car.

It seemed Tre was getting the best of him, and Bank was almost out of bullets he carefully placed

Jewel's motionless body in the passenger seat still trying to aim toward his target.

"Stay with me baby girl. Stay with me" Bank whispered.

He made his way to the driver side as he noticed Siren laying there lifeless with the bag of money and his care gone. He didn't even notice Tati making her exist with his money.

Tre, still firing his gun, walked smoothly toward Bank's car. "It's over my nigga."

Pow! Pow!

In an instant, Tre fell to his knees.

Pow! Pow!

Two more shots, this time to the head to finish the job. Juan walked over to his victim and stood over Tre's lifeless body to confirm he was dead. He looked at both men dead in front of him and made his way to Bankroll's car.

"Go handle your business fam," Juan said.

"Appreciate it," Bank said.

He could hear a small moan coming from Jewel next to him. She was slumped over and blood was everywhere. She could feel her life slipping away, but the sound of her moans let Bank know she was still holding on.

"Just hold on baby, I'm going to take care of you," Bank said, stilling showing the same emotions he had for her.

"Bank?" Jewel said forcefully.

"Don't speak bae. Save your energy," Bank said.

Jewel continues to moan in pain. She could feel her heart beating through her chest. "There's… no.. baby Bank," Jewel confessed.

Bank shut his eyes for a select second as he held his composure together. A small tear dropped from his as he thought about the pain and hurt he's been through. Over the last few days he r alone he really loved Jewel and could stomach the thought of her hurting him

"It's okay bae. Don't speak on that. Just rest," Bank said.

When he notices that she is no longer responding or even moaning he looks toward her. Her eyes wide open with her head against the window. Jewel took her last breath.

The End

www.ingramcontent.com/pod-product-compliance
Lightning Source LLC
Chambersburg PA
CBHW061245120726
48001CB00001B/148